Even More Wifey Status:

Renaissance Collection

Even More Wifey Status:

Renaissance Collection

Racquel Williams

www.urbanbooks.net

Urban Books, LLC
300 Farmingdale Road, NY-Route 109
Farmingdale, NY 11735

Even More Wifey Status: Renaissance Collection
Copyright © 2018 Racquel Williams

ISBN 13: 978-1-62286-676-2
ISBN 10: 1-62286-676-2

First Mass Market Printing February 2018
Printed in the United States of America

10 9 8 7 6 5 4 3 2 1

This is a work of fiction. Any references or similarities to actual events, real people, living or dead, or to real locales are intended to give the novel a sense of reality. Any similarity in other names, characters, places, and incidents is entirely coincidental.

Distributed by Kensington Publishing Corp.
Submit orders to:
Customer Service
400 Hahn Road
Westminster, MD 21157-4627
Phone: 1-800-733-3000
Fax: 1-800-659-243

Even More Wifey Status:

Renaissance Collection

Racquel Williams

Dedication

I dedicate this book to my three sons: Malik, Jehmel, and Zahir. I love you guys with everything in me. Words cannot explain how much I love y'all. So I will let my actions lead the way.

Acknowledgments

First and foremost, I want to give all praises to Allah. He has brought me through so many obstacles and continues to bless me every day.

To my mom, Rosa, thanks for being there through everything. I am forever grateful.

To my husband, Carlo, thank you for supporting me and working your tail off so I can be a full-time writer. I love you.

To my bestie, Sophia. Words cannot explain the bond we share. I love you, twenty-six years and counting.

To Papaya, Ebonee, Charmaine, and Stacey: thank you guys for being there for me as I tread on this journey. I love y'all.

To my big brothers, Author Blacc Topp, Mr. Chronic Black, and Thomas Long. I'm so happy to have you guys in my life. I am grateful that our paths crossed. Keep grinding, the world's watching.

Special shout-out to the Literary Divas of Spartanburg Book Club. Thanks for giving a new author a chance. I love you guys.

Special thanks to my editor, Tyresha; I am forever grateful.

Special shout-out to Blacc Topp's Round Table and Faye Wilkes for supporting me and giving me the chance I needed to reach new readers. I am forever grateful.

Shout-out to Slyce Book Club, DJ Gatsby Book Club, New Author Showcase, and My Urban Book Club for their support.

To Makey, thank you for being there when I needed an ear, without judgment. I love you!

To Nola, Beverly, Melloney, Rhea, Trina, Nikki Blue, Nikki Macnificent, Teri, Rosslyn, Mita, Kendra, Lisa, Angela, Natasha, Arlena, Nawlinz, Nikki Williams, Anita, Stephanie, Kathleen, Christina, Deborah, Judy, Evelyn, Phyllis, Sharlene, and Mama Joyce, I want to say thank-you, guys, for being there since I started my journey. If no one supports me, I know I can count on y'all. I am definitely blessed.

To Toya, big up yourself. Friends for life.

To my Black Destiny Publications family, I appreciate all the hard work and dedication. We are moving forward to greater things. Stay focused.

Acknowledgments

To my family in the U.S., Jamaica, Canada, and England—too many to name, but you know who you are. Thanks for the love and support.

To Christopher Lee, you already know the love is real. This is your year coming up!

To all the brothers and sisters on lock, stay down. There *is* light at the end of the darkness.

Special shout-out to all my readers and supporters—too many to name. I appreciate all the support. I am forever grateful.

Shout-out to Gregory Graphics. You did a great job on my cover.

To everyone that I failed to mention, charge it to my head and not my heart.

Prologue

I used to listen to people speak of how close they came to death during a trauma, and how their spirits left their bodies and wandered off. Truth be told, I used to laugh in their faces and call them liars. That was . . . until I experienced it on my own.

Here I was in an unfamiliar place with a bunch of familiar faces, laughing and hugging me, like I was the prodigal child that finally made it home. My eyes wandered around as I was looking to see my man or even that crackhead bitch of a mother, but they were not there. A feeling of emptiness came over me, and tears trickled down my face. I felt desperate at that moment. Then an old white-haired lady approached me out of nowhere. Her face seemed familiar, but I could not place it. She stepped toward me and gave me the warmest smile. It sent chills through my frail body. I could not help but smile right back at her.

"Grandbaby, you're here. How are you feeling?" she asked and stretched her hands out and touched my face.

It was at that moment that I remembered her face. She was my grandmother who died before I was born. My first encounter with her spirit was a few months back when I was going through hard times dealing with Alijah's situation.

"I know you feel scared and must be wondering where you are."

"Yes, where am I? How did all these people get here, and why does everybody seem to be all happy and geeking? Aren't you supposed to be dead?"

"Relax, honey. This is the other side. You were in a serious accident, and you crossed over. Everyone's here to welcome you so your transformation will go smoothly."

"Welcome me? What the heck you mean? Am I dead?" I looked at her for some type of response.

"No, darling, you are not dead yet. Your spirit just traveled off searching for a new home. Your body is still in the hospital. Those doctors are working their tails off trying to keep you alive."

"Grandma, I feel so tired. My body hurts, and I just want to lie down for a little bit. I-I can't think. I just need to rest," I pleaded.

"Don't you talk like that, child. You have a lot of unfinished business left to handle," she said in a fierce tone.

"I can't. I feel so weak."

"Listen, chile, you are a Rogers, and you're coming from a strong bloodline of women. You will fight. Dry them darn tears and go on back over. When it's your time to come back, I will be right here waiting on you with open arms."

Before I could respond, she disappeared, and all the other people were gone in a split second. I was left standing alone in complete darkness.

"We have a pulse! Get in here! She's breathing!" I heard a voice shouting.

There was a lot of noise around me, and a tall white man was standing over me. "Welcome back, little lady. I thought I lost you for a second, but I see you are a fighter."

I was too weak to respond, so I nodded my head and closed my eyes. I needed to rest and could not wait a minute longer!

Chapter One

Alijah Jackson

The happiness of being released from jail was short lived. I knew Sierra did not like Shayna and shit. I could dig it, but this was some totally different shit when she came at me telling me that Shayna was the one who snitched on me.

They said seeing was believing, so I had no choice but to believe what the fuck was in front of me in bold print. *"Shayna Jackson, Confidential Informant."* See, I was a street nigga, so I'm used to niggas hating and snitching, but that was a whole different part of the game. My mind was racing. I felt like my blood was boiling. My vein felt like it was about to burst through my forehead. I just kept repeating that bitch's name over and over . . . I jumped off the bed and threw the papers against the wall. But before I could get another thought in, I heard gunshots in my house.

Pop, Pop, Pop!

Next, I heard Sierra screaming my name.

I raced to my closet where I usually kept my guns, but the closet was empty. I didn't have time to look elsewhere. I had to get my baby girl, even though I didn't have a gun. Fuck it, I was ready for whatever or whoever. I ran out into the hallway without drawers, dick hanging.

"Sierra! Where the fuck are you?" I yelled with nervousness in my voice.

There was no need for an answer. Sierra lay by the door in a pool of blood. I looked around to make sure no one was in the house. I ran upstairs and grabbed my cell and a blanket and dialed 9-1-1. Then I ran back downstairs and checked her pulse. She was still breathing so I began to put pressure on the area where I saw the blood coming from.

"Hello, 9-1-1. What's your emergency?"

"I need an ambulance. My girl has been shot. Blood is everywhere. Please hurry."

I gave the operator the address. I could not explain how I was feeling because I had no feelings at all.

"OK, sir, where is she shot?"

"I think in the chest. I'm not sure."

"Emergency help is on the way. In the meantime, I need some information from you. What is her name, age, and your name, sir?"

"Yo, bitch. No disrespect, just send the fucking ambulance. 'Cause if she don't make it, I'm coming for you."

"Sir, there's no need for the name-calling. I'm just doing my job. I need to enter this information into the system, and you being ignorant is not helping the situation."

"Bitch, shut the fuck up! Where is the fucking ambulance? My bitch is on the fucking floor dying, and you think I give a fuck about how I'm actin'?"

Before I could finish my sentence, I heard the ambulance pulling up. I let go of Sierra's hand and threw on the boxers that I grabbed off the bed. I then ran outside to get their attention. Within seconds, my house was swarmed with emergency workers and five-O. That was not the place I wanted to be, but I had no choice because I wasn't leaving her side.

Shayna Jackson

Bitches thought I was a joke when I said, "I am the head bitch in charge." Hell, nah! I meant that shit. I would not be pushed or run over. I run this, and it was that simple.

I knew I was losing Alijah, and I couldn't risk that. It wasn't that I wanted that no-good, two-timing-ass nigga, but I want his fucking money. *I'm* Mrs. Jackson, and I'll be damned if that ghetto-ass bitch was going to weasel her way into his life. I called up her best friend. I almost choked saying that. Okay, I called up her childhood friend, ace, road dawg—whatever name you want to call it—so I could get the address. I didn't trust that crackhead bitch, but she was a valuable source to have, especially when I gave her greedy ass a couple of hundred dollars and got classified information. With a friend like that, who needed a fucking enemy?

I was so thankful to Daddy. When I was a little girl, every Saturday morning, he would take me along with him to the shooting range. Being a retired military man, he always warned me about the importance of the right to bear arms. I did not know twenty years later that I would be exercising my right to bear arms against my husband.

I really thought that all my problems were over after the cops picked up Alijah and his cronies, so I got a new phone and stayed glued to my television. The local CBS station picked up the news about the fall of one of Richmond's drug lords. I was beyond pleased at how fast the authorities scooped them all up. I was too caught up in the moment that I did not realize that they did not lock up that bitch. That's a shame because I knew I would have to handle her personally now. What's wrong with these fucking cops? They should've done their job. Now I had to get my hands dirty. Well, sometimes the *boss* had to do the dirty work.

"Hello, ma'am, welcome to South Side Guns and Things."

"Hello, I'm looking for a gun. Something powerful, you know?"

"Well, you're in the right place. I have a variety of powerful guns that might suit you, pretty little lady." He smiled at me showing those dirty things in his mouth. I needed to hurry up and get away from this bum.

He showed me a variety of guns. I decided to go along with the Glock 9 mm. Just holding it in my hands gave my pussy a certain sensation. I felt tingly, so I knew the Glock was the one for me. I gave him my fake ID and information; then I walked out with my weapon tucked away in my Michael Kors purse. I took my shades off and started down the street, pulling off my red wig, letting my hair down as I drove off into the brisk air.

Chapter Two

Sierra Rogers

I'd been in the hospital over two weeks, and I recovered quickly. I was told that I almost didn't make it, so I was grateful that God gave me another chance at life. I was shocked when I found out that I was pregnant, but I also was happy. Maybe now I would not feel so all alone in this world. I have someone to love and care for. Sadness also came over me. Alijah was my child's father, and he was in the streets heavy. I was not sure where we were heading. After all, it was his drama that caused me to end up in the hospital fighting for my life. All different types of thoughts ran through my mind, and I don't know how it's going to be played out. I just know everybody's going to be paid in full, but in due time. There's no need to rush; first things first. I needed my strength back, and then everything else will fall in place.

Alijah's been very supportive. He's barely left the hospital. He kept apologizing to me. He felt guilty that he was not there to protect me, and I knew he would have, but who would've ever imagined that I would get shot in a gated community? Oh well, that shows that evil is everywhere, even on my own doorsteps. He was also excited about the baby; even more excited than I appeared to be sometimes. He's hoping for a boy, but deep down, I was hoping for a "mini-me." I did not want a son to follow in his father's footsteps. I would fuck a dope boy, marry a dope boy, but I surely don't want my son to become a dope boy. It might not make sense, but it is a big difference when it's your man. I have seen too many mothers on their knees bawling for their seeds. I know I'm a strong person, but that was one pain that I do not—and I repeat—do *not* want to bear.

Li'l Mo' was also at the hospital with me daily. She even hooked up my hair, saying I looked a damn mess. I had to laugh at my bestie. She came in my life at a point when I needed someone, and she's been with me ever since. I thought our relationship would have taken a wrong turn after we slept together, but truthfully, I think it brought us closer. Not because of our secret, but because when times got hard, we always had each other's back and front. I couldn't imagine my life without her in it.

Tears welled up in my eyes as I think back on the bond Neisha and I used to share. How did we get to this point . . . What went wrong? I was confused. I remembered our last interaction at my house, and I had to whoop that ass. I didn't feel good about it. We'd been friends since birth, went through everything together, and this was how it turned out. The sad part about it, from what I heard, she was high on dope. I have no understanding why a brilliant girl with a promising future would make that decision. She saw my mother; she was there with me and knows the effects of drugs. I snapped back into reality and reminded myself that she was no longer the little girl that was my best friend. We're long past that. I couldn't let my emotions get involved when dealing with a snake. Snakes comes in all forms and sizes, and from that point on, I decided to keep my grass cut low until I find out who set me up and who gave that bitch my address. When I find out, they will be dealt with as *the bottom bitch rises!*

Alijah Jackson

I knew that I was a born killer from the time that I was growing up in Tivoli Gardens. I used to feel a rush of excitement overcome me whenever there were turf wars, and niggas were getting killed. I remembered the first time I killed someone. I was overcome with joy inside as I watched the bullets enter the nigga. Some might've considered me sick, but in my world, it's either you are the hunter, or you can fuck around and become the hunted. I decided to become the hunter. I would kill from age five to eighty-five if I felt like you haven't been loyal. People were born with loyalty; it can't be learned. The first time that I sensed any type of disloyalty, I'd put my Glock to the head and pull the trigger without even blinking. Yes, I was a born killer.

After Sierra got shot, I felt like my manhood was tested. I've been racking my brain as to who would be that fucking bold to enter a man's house—not just any regular man, but *my* house, *my* fucking domain. Sierra wasn't of any help and couldn't remember who shot her. At times, I tended to go hard on her trying to help her remember. The doctor explained to me that when people go through such a horrific trauma, sometimes they block out events leading to the tragedy. That's why she couldn't remember. I needed to fucking know who did it, however. This was personal. She was carrying my seed, and any crime against her was a crime against my seed. I vowed to find out who it was, and I wouldn't shoot them—instead, I'd slowly torture them with my hands.

I typically stayed at the top of my game, but I see that I wasn't. I had two snakes on my team, and I kept racking my brain. How I did not sense that Shayna and Markus were fucking with my dough was beyond me. And to think the nigga was also fucking my wife! I didn't give a fuck if it was only on paper; that ho belonged to me. The nigga thought he could fuck my ho *and* steal my dough? Hell, nah! That's why he paid with his life. In my world, it's death before dishonor. Now on to the ho that was behind it all, I'm still shocked that this ho was a snake all along. I had to admit that she played her cards right, because I did not see this coming. Only difference with me and her, I'm going to make sure she *see* me coming. I planned to torture that bitch like I never even knew her. No more Mr. Nice Guy. I was out to get blood. Babies, children, mommas and daddies, if anyone get in my way, I'm going to slaughter them. I was the new fucking sheriff in town, and it's either bow down or get killed!

I drove over to Fairfield to meet up with Saleem. I had some serious business to handle, and he was the man that could help me. Chuck and Dre also met up with us. It was a good feeling to have my homies all together again. God knows my heart still hurts from missing Darryl. I wish I could go back and change the hands of time, but I knew that was not reality. I could only look out for his seed once he's born and make sure he's well taken care of. If the shoe was on the other foot, I know he would do the same for me, without a doubt.

"What's up, fellas?" I greeted them, and we exchanged dap.

"No need to wonder what the emergency is. It's been two weeks since Sierra got touched and still no leads. Y'all know sey my 'oman dat and a pussy come in my place and hurt her. I don't need no bloodclaat Babylon pon dis. This is a personal beef, and it need to be dealt wit' ASAP!"

"I hear you, boss. We ready for whatever and whoever. Just say the word, we riding," Chuck assured me.

"You know, brotha, this some weird shit. No one in the street talkin'. It's like a fucking mystery. I am dumbfounded on this one. Trust me, I have connections in these streets and not one lead. This some big shit," Saleem said while shaking his head in confusion.

"I hear what the fuck y'all saying. But I can't fucking eat, sleep, or can't comfortably sit on the toilet and shit until I know who is behind this. Bottom line is when *I* start feeling uncomfortable, *e'erybody* goin' feel the wrath of my gun—no bullshit. Me a di real big man 'round here, and a pussy just try me. I need a fucking name!"

I never cried in front of my niggas, but I was fuming with anger. I wanted to kill everyone in this whole fucking town. Trust me, they had no idea who the fuck they were playing with. Saleem walked beside me and placed his arm on my shoulder.

"Brother man, humble yourself. I would feel the same way you do, but like I always tell you, you cannot act off impulse. You just came home, and these pigs still watching you. They upset that you got off, so they in the cut waiting on you to fuck up. You a warrior. You need to humble yourself and think out your plan, but first you have to find out who the enemy is, and then deal with them accordingly."

"I hear you, bro, and no disrespect, but I am not understanding right now. I need to know— better yet, get the word out that I'm putting up a million-dollar reward for any info on the shooting. I bet somebody will open their fucking mouth then."

"Bet. I will put out the word ASAP. My peoples will also keep their ears to the streets."

"I appreciate it, fellas. I got to get to the hospital; check on my girl and my seed." I jumped in my truck and sped off. My mind continued to race. All kinds of evil thoughts were circulated in my brain, and I needed a quick fix.

Chapter Three

Sierra Rogers

I was released from the hospital and was happy as hell. I was about tired of all the doctors and nurses, claiming they taking blood and checking blood pressure all hours of the night. Don't get me wrong, I appreciated them for saving my life, but I had to go. I had things to deal with. The part that bugged me out is the constant questioning about me getting my memory back of the shooting. I done told their asses a million and one times that I did not see who shot me, and if I did, I couldn't remember. I tried to convince Alijah, but he asked me the same damn question every day. The other day I had to snap on his ass. Hopefully, he'll leave it alone now.

Alijah asked me if I wanted a new house because of what happened there. I told him no. This was my house, and just because a bitch wanted to show her ass, I was not going to up and leave my shit. That was not my reason for staying. My reason was I needed to be there so it can be a reminder to me of what happened there—motivate me to get that bitch back one way or another.

It felt so good to be back in my own king-size bed. Boy, I sure missed living like a queen. My wound was healing well, and I was getting all my strength back. I had an appointment with the hospital OB-GYN, and he told me my baby was just fine. Sometimes I had to rub my stomach and make a mental note that I was going to be a mother.

I knew it was rough on Li'l Mo' running the shop by herself, but she hired another stylist to help out while I was away. I cannot even say how much this chick has done for me, but she was definitely a blessing.

I woke up from a much-needed rest. I was still taking Percocet for the pain, and, boy, it had me floating on cloud nine. I got up to use the restroom, and when I did, I heard a male and a female voice coming from downstairs, so I walked down to investigate. I entered the living room and saw Alijah sitting down talking to a woman whose back was turned to me. I guess I interrupted their conversation because suddenly Alijah turned his attention to me.

"Hey, babe, thought you were still asleep," he said with a nervous grin plastered across his face.

Before I could respond, the woman stood up and turned around and faced me. I blinked twice. I really thought that it was a joke. Shit, I thought it was the Percocet fucking with my mind, but, nah, it was not. It was my crack-smoking mother that left me when I was a child now standing in my living room looking like she'd just won the fucking mother-of-the-year trophy.

"What the fuck is this bitch doing in my house?" I asked with venom in my voice.

"Ma, calm down. I went and found her after you got shot. I thought she needed to know about what happened to you."

I did not get a chance to respond before this bitch spoke up.

"Baby, he only meant well, and I had to come see you, you know." She stepped closer and stretched her hand out to touch me. I slapped her hand away.

I took a step back so I could gather my thoughts before I let this bitch know how I really felt.

"Listen, you crackhead bitch, I am not your fucking baby. I am a grown-ass woman and don't you come in my shit acting all high and fucking mighty. You chose a glass dick over your only seed, and now you in my fucking face. Bitch, I didn't fucking need you when I was young, and I damn sure don't need your raggedy ass now."

I then turned back toward Alijah and dug into his ass.

"Alijah, the next time you want to play captain save a ho, you do it on your own damn time. I did not ask you to meddle in my fucking life. I never wanted to see this bitch again, but you brought it up on yourself."

"Yo, who the fuck you talkin' to? Calm yourself. At the end of the fucking day, it's your moms, so chill out and stop getting yourself so riled up. It might be a good thing for both of you to get to know each other again."

"He's right, Sierra. Trust me, I understand how you feel, and I cannot blame you because I was a piece-of-shit mother. I treated you bad, and I can't make no excuse, but I been clean for two years now, and I'm in a program that helps me. Please understand that I want to be in your life," she pleaded.

I had so much anger in me that I stormed toward that bitch. I knew my health was not in the best shape, but I just wanted to shut that bitch up. I could not stand there and listen to her talk about how she was clean or what the fuck that should matter to me. I was a grown woman, and I could care less if she was still fucking and sucking every trick dick that came along. I have been so over her and that fucked-up-ass life. If she only knew how much I hated her.

I pushed that bitch on the couch, but before I could do anything else, Alijah jumped in the middle and grabbed my arm with a tight grip.

"Yo, B, you fucking crazy? Don't you ever put your hands on your mom. I don't give a fuck what she did to you. Certain shit you just don't do. You hear me? You really acting out right now, trying to fight with my seed in your stomach. You definitely trippin'."

"Man, let go of my fucking arm. Whose side you on anyway? You taking up for this crackhead bitch that you don't even know? Are you fucking serious? *I* am your woman, you hear me?" I said with tears rolling down my cheeks.

"Alijah, you shouldn't have stopped her. I deserve everything that she is dishing out. I can handle it. Trust me, I am stronger than I appear. When I decided to come here, I knew what to expect. She is my daughter, and I've known how strong she was ever since she was a little girl," the crackhead bitch spoke up.

"Listen up. I know my woman is hurting, so you don't get no fucking medal. You fucked her life up, and she's hurting, but I tell you what . . . If you still on crack or you trying to disappear out of her life again, best bet is to do it now. Because if you ever—and I repeat—*ever* hurt her again, they going to find your body at the bottom of the James River. And I don't make threats; I make promises," Alijah warned.

"Ain't no need to do all that. I never want to see this bitch ever again. She need to go back to whatever hole she crawled out of because I have no use for her crackhead, hoish ass. Get the fuck out of my house!"

"Sierra, I'm not going to be too many more bitches and hoes. I know I fucked up, but you not gon' keep calling me all those damn names. Now, *I'm* the fucking mama, and *you* the child, so watch your mouth before it gets real serious in here."

"Bitch, what? You a fucking joke. Threaten me and fuck around get killed. I would not care less if you are the bitch that spit me outta your pussy. I fucking hated you when I was fifteen, and I hate you with a passion this fucking moment."

I saw the disgusted look on Alijah's face as if he wasn't feeling this showdown. Hell, I could care less. He was the one that went and dug this bitch out of her hole and brought her to my fucking house. I wish I knew what was going on in his head.

"You know, I tried. Alijah knows where to reach me. Whenever you want to address this like two grown women should do, then you call me. Other than that, I am leaving your selfish, spoiled ass alone."

"*Spoiled?* Did I hear you right? You left me alone to fend for my fucking self. I had to fuck and suck dope boys just to keep a fucking roof over my head and food on my table. I was raped and left for dead by one of your tricks, and you call *me* selfish? Bitch, you don't know the half of it."

I guessed I hit a nerve because this bitch ran out the front door, and I ran upstairs and locked the bedroom door leaving Alijah's ass standing there with a dumb-ass look on his face. This was the first time that he heard all the things that I blurted out. Too bad. I knew he knew that I was damaged mentally.

I lay on the bed with my head buried underneath one of my pillows. I cried so hard, I felt like my chest was ripping into pieces. All the pain that I buried inside was coming out, and I could not stop it, nor did I want to. I had years of pain bottled up in me, and I needed to let it out.

I heard Alijah banging on the door, but I told him to go away. I just wanted to be alone. This was a battle that I had to fight alone and didn't know where to start. All I knew was my life has been hell ever since I, Sierra Rogers, entered this wicked world.

Shayna Jackson

See, Alijah fucked up when he tried to play me. I was a good woman when he met me. All I ever wanted was someone to love and lace me with their money. I did not want a man that slung his dick up in all these ghetto-ass bitches. I just couldn't understand how he had a woman with education and class; a woman that came from a good family with a great background—and he didn't want that. Instead, he chose to go after that poor-ass project bitch that doesn't even have a pot to piss in. He straight up disrespected me, and I will not tolerate that type of disrespect coming from a street nigga.

I had no choice but to hurt the bitch that he loved. I made a vow a long time ago that if I could not have him, nobody else would, and I meant that. Earlier that evening, I found out that all charges were dropped against him and his cronies, and I almost hit the roof. All the fucking evidence I gave them, and they let this nigga walk. This shit was definitely unheard of in my book. I was so fucking pissed that I hung up on that Uncle Tom-ass nigga. Here I was putting my life on the line and hand this nigga over to them with evidence, and they screw around and let him loose. I really hope he didn't know that it was me that turned on him, because I knew what he's capable of doing. I thought about leaving the country, but I decided not to. I had a lot of business to handle. I was going to show Alijah and his bitch that I was the HBIC!

I had a few loose ends to tie up, so after I handled his bitch, I called her friend to have a talk with her. We decided to meet up in a secluded area. I couldn't risk being seen with this bitch. I sat in my car waited for that bitch to pull up in the same old hoopty that she had before. I directed her to get in my car, and, boy, what a mistake that was. The bitch smelled like stale urine and looked like she hadn't bathed in weeks. I had to roll my window down so some fresh air could come in my car.

"Listen up, I called this meeting because some serious shit went down. And I wanted to make sure that you have not been running your mouth about anything concerning me and the information that you gave me."

"No, what happen? I never mentioned your name about anything, and how serious is this shit you talkin' about? I can't get mixed up in no drama."

"Listen, you don't need no information. As long as you keep your mouth shut, everything will be fine. Remember, this can be life or death. You decide which one you want. Here's five grand. Take it and disappear. Get out of my life. I won't contact you ever again, and remember, we've never met." I handed her the envelope of cash. I was also careful to use a glove.

"God bless you. I won't say a word, and your secret is safe with me. I promise."

"Okay, now, get your ass out of my car. And you should try showering. Your stench is horrible." I motioned for her to get out of my car immediately.

"You are so rude. Maybe that's why your man ran into the arms of another woman. You should try working on your attitude," she said, gritting on me.

"Listen up, you little dopefiend bitch, you in the wrong league. Don't let me show you who you fucking with like I had to show your little friend. Now get your stinking ass out of my ride before I blow your fucking brains out." I gave her a final warning.

She must've got the drift because she exited the car mumbling something underneath her bad breath. I got some disinfectant wipes off the backseat and wiped my leather seat off. I then sprayed my car with Lysol deodorizer.

I looked around to make sure no one saw me. Then I sped through the empty parking lot. I really pray that bitch kept her mouth shut or I would have to shut it for her. God knew I was traveling down the wrong path, but if this is what it takes to secure my place in Alijah's pockets, then it's all worth the sacrifice.

I dialed Sanders's number. It's about time we have a real talk.

"Hello, Sanders, this is Mrs. Jackson. We need to talk ASAP."

"Well, I'm working on a case right now and will be in the office all day."

"All right, well, after dark is just fine. We can meet in my hotel room. I'll order us dinner and a nightcap."

"Hmm, sounds interesting. I'll be there around eight," he replied with a devilish grin.

"OK, see you then, Sanders," I replied, and then chuckled.

I gave him my hotel info before I hung up the phone. I was familiar with men like him. They think they can fuck every sexy woman that comes their way, but he's not used to *my* type of woman. I will find a man like him, stroke his ego, get on my knees, and suck the black or the white off his cock, and then I will get on top and ride his cock until he busts. When it's all said and done, I will have him where I want him, and then before he realizes it, I'll manipulate him like a puppet on a string.

I ran some errands and got back to my hotel just in time to shower and get myself ready to meet the man in charge of the Richmond PD. I knew that I was playing with fire, but I would not be me if I did not take a chance.

I ordered us a nice dinner so we could sit and enjoy our meal and drink wine. This type of thing was not new to me, but it was a new victim. What I knew was that all men are dogs, and they always thought with their lower head. My thoughts were interrupted when I heard a hard knock on the door. I jumped up and walked over and opened the door.

"Hello, Sanders, welcome to my little nest," I said jokingly.

"Shayna, thank you for inviting me."

Honestly, he was not a bad-looking man. He was tall, had dark skin, a little on the heavy side, but nevertheless, he was still easy on the eyes. We sat at the table and had our dinner which I ordered; steak and potatoes with vegetables on the side. I knew he'd appreciate this type of meal accompanied by a beautiful woman.

After about three glasses of red wine, I excused myself from the table and went to the ladies' room. I took off all my clothes and left only my heels on. Then I pranced back in the room where I interrupted him looking down on his cell phone. He quickly looked up, and it was then he realized that I was standing in front of him naked as the day my momma gave birth to me. I could tell by his long stare that he was surprised. I walked over to him and started loosening his tie with one hand, while I grabbed his balls with the other.

"Ouch, take it easy down there. These things are delicate, you know," he said while letting out a long moan.

I knew he was getting aroused. His cock was standing firm in his drawers. I led him over to the queen-sized bed and pushed him down on his back. This was easier than I thought. I unbuttoned his pants and pulled his legs out with his help. I then got on my knees on the carpet, looked him in the eyes like I was in love with him, licked my lips, and kissed the tip of his cock. Even though I didn't love this lame-ass nigga, I sure love me a big cock. I allowed my lips to slide over his dark caramel cock. I had to close my eyes to keep myself from laughing and let out one of my signature fake moans, just to let him know I was doing this for my pleasure. I sucked his cock head into my mouth and allowed my tongue to tease the tip. I opened my eyes and looked up at him in my sexiest I-love-your-cock look. This nigga had his eyes closed, mouth wide open, moaning like a bitch. As soon as my inner Superhead was starting to come out, I felt this nigga's hand gripping my hair with force.

"Ouch! No, no."

However, he did not stop. He pulled me up off my knees, so I stood up with him, looked him dead in the eyes, and thought to myself, *This is how you wanna play it?* I gave him a wicked smile, smacked him across the face, and pushed him against the wall. I turned around and took his cock in my hand, bent over, and took his cock head and rubbed from my clit upward until it got right at my pussy hole. I eased myself back on it just a little, looked back at him a little, taunting him. Just as if he was on command, he grabbed my hips. I could feel him pushing his hard black cock into my wet, high-maintenance pussy. He had no idea that this was my way of getting him into my world of madness and mayhem.

He was stroking me, and I was throwing my ass back on him. I could admit this man had a big-ass cock, the type that can fill up the hole. I was enjoying myself a little too much. I had to regroup because I did not want to lose focus on the reason why he was in my hotel room in the first place.

He slid his cock out and turned me around, picked me up, and threw me on the bed. He quickly spread my legs apart and slid his cock into my slippery wet hole. It was at that moment I felt the full wrath of his manhood. This was my cue to get it in, so I started to scream bloody murder. The more I screamed, the harder he fucked me.

"No! No! Why you doing this to me?"

"Baby, this is what you wanted. You asked for this cock, now open up and take it."

"I can't. I don't want to. Stop!" I pleaded.

"I got you; just hold me. You asked for it, and I'm giving it to you. Oh shit, this pussy is so fucking wet. Damn, woman, I need this."

"I'm sorry, please stop. I can't—please," I mumbled with tears rolling down my face.

"I love it when you beg me. You know how to turn a man on, and I'm about to bust. *Aargh, aargh!*"

This fool done came all in my pussy. I got up and ran to the bathroom, where I got my Ziploc bag and let his come slowly drain out. I then took a swab and wiped my pussy and put both in a Ziploc bag and sealed it. Quickly, I placed it in my dirty clothes basket. I had to get it to my refrigerator as soon as this fool left. I slightly washed off, washed my hands, then I walked back in the room with tears rolling down my face. This nigga was lying on his back with a stupid grin plastered across his face along with his soft, wrinkled dick.

"Hi, babe, how was it?"

"I need you to go. I just want to be alone," I demanded.

"Damn, woman, you just used me, and then send me on my way?"

"I said get out. I just want to be alone," I said and threw his clothes at him.

"Wow! Talk about split personalities. You need to get your ass checked. I know the dick is good, but I don't think it should make you act like *this*."

I did not entertain that fool. I sat on the bed whimpering and shaking. I watched as he got dressed and left my room. I jumped up and wiped away my fucking tears. I should win the fucking trophy-of-the-year award, because that there was one of the best performances I've ever given. I made sure the door was locked and stripped the sheets off the bed, but not before I grabbed my recorder from under the pillow. I went to the bathroom and got my package and placed it in the refrigerator. Then I poured me a glass of wine and sat in my chair with the tape recorder in hand and thinking of my next big move.

Chapter Four

Sierra Rogers

It's crazy how our lives can change in the blink of an eye. One minute I was getting my man out of jail, and the next minute, I had a gun pointed in my face. I had a guardian angel watching over me that night, because out of the four shots that were fired, only one hit me. I could only give praise to the Man Above.

Li'l Mo' was on her way over. This was our first time chilling since I had been feeling better, so I was amped to see my right-hand bitch. We had so much to catch up on, and I definitely had things that I wanted to share with her. I knew she had my best interest at heart, and she was the only one that I could confide in.

I heard the doorbell ring, and this time, I checked the peephole so I could see who was standing there. That bitch caught me slipping once. It wouldn't happen a second time. It was Mo' at the door, so I opened it.

She stepped in, and we greeted each other with a hug. We held on to each other for a good minute. No words were needed; our long embrace explained it all. We finally let go and walked toward the living room. I knew she brought me some weed, even though I shouldn't be smoking, and Alijah would have a fit if he ever found out that Mo' brought me some. He already did not like her, and this would only make it worse.

"I already rolled up so we can hit it real fast. You know your daddy might catch us," she said jokingly while she took out a blunt and lit it up.

"Yea, come on, then. Puff, puff, pass that ganja, gyal," I said in my best imitation of Alijah's accent.

"Look at you, still greedy as hell. Ain't nothin' change."

We busted out laughing. These were the days that I missed, good old laughter with my ace. She passed me the blunt, and I hurriedly put it to my mouth like a dopefiend smoking that pipe. I missed smoking on some good herb. I took a few more pulls and gave it back; we ended up smoking the entire thing. I then went and brushed my teeth, put a few drops of Visine in my eyes, sprayed the room, and changed my clothes. I didn't want Alijah to find out what I was doing behind his back.

"So how you feeling?" Mo' inquired.

"I'm feeling much better. The pain is not as bad as it used to be. I am definitely getting my strength back."

"So I never got a chance to hear the full story of what happened. I only got bits and pieces from Alijah."

I sat beside her and told her everything that went down earlier in the day. I did not mention what I had to do to get Alijah out of jail. That was between Charles and I, and I will take that to my grave. I then told her about what happened after we got home, and I finished the story off about opening the door and getting shot.

"So, did you see who shot you?"

At that moment I wanted to lie to her, but I could not. We've been through too much.

"Listen, Mo', you my ace, so what I'm about to tell you is in confidence. You cannot tell this to anyone. You hear me, *no one*." I looked her dead in the eyes so she could know how serious this was.

"Damn, bitch, you acting like it's top secret. And why the fuck you haven't said anything before? You kno' your man wants to know."

"Okay, it was that bitch-ass Shayna. *She* shot me."

"You are fucking playing, right?"

"I am dead-ass serious. That bitch was standing on my doorstep with a gun in her hand aimed at me."

"So, what I don't understand is why didn't you tell the cops or Alijah."

"I did not want them to know. This bitch violated him. She transgressed against my ass, and I want to show her that I'm not to be fucked with."

"Really? So how you plan on doing that?" she asked with a curious look plastered on her face.

"The less you know, the better it will be for you. I don't want you to get mixed up in this; plus, I need my baby's godmother to be straight from all this mess."

"Bitch, spare me the speech. I am riding *for* you, *with* you, regardless. I just want you to think this out first. Don't make no fucked-up moves. I'm here if you need me."

"I know you got me, and I appreciate that, but this is something that I have to handle on my own. I think about this bitch every fuckin' second, and it's driving me crazy. I *have* to settle the score. Just trust me on this one, please?" I looked at her with tears in my eyes.

"I got you, boo. We are like sisters, and I would not be able to live with myself if anything ever happened to you. Just be careful, you hear me?" she said, grabbing my arm.

"You trippin', bitch. You actin' like I'm going to die. I have nine lives like a cat. Plus, I have to be here to raise my baby. I promise you that," I assured her as I squeezed her hand.

I then got up and walked to the window. I did not want her to see the long tears rolling down my face. The truth was, I had no idea how this was going to play out. I didn't even know where to start. I knew I had to get this bitch back. I had to make her pay for all the drama that she put me through. How it's going to end, only God knows the answer.

I dried my tears and walked back to the couch. I changed the story and gave her an update on my mother coming over to the house. We talked for a little while longer; then she left. I wanted her to stay, to lay in her arms. I wanted her to run her fingers through my hair and tell me it's going to be a'ight, but the time wasn't right, and Alijah could've popped up at any minute.

Alijah Jackson

My life was turned upside down. The police wanted to lock me up for life, Creighton niggas wanted my head, and that ho I married was a fucking snitch. God knew I had enemies coming from all angles. I had to figure a way to stay alive and free. I was about to become a father, and I could not risk not being there to see my blood. I was ready for war. I had to live no matter what situation presented itself. I thought about moving my family out of town, maybe go back up top, but I had too much money tied up in VA, and the timing was off. I knew I was under the pigs' radar, but I planned on staying out of the way for a minute. My lawyer told me to lie low because he was not sure why the charges were dropped. Every street nigga knew that nine times out of ten, when the state drop the case, the feds usually pick it up. I wasn't going to just sit back and let them come get me. I was going to go hard for a few months, tie up all my affairs, and then bounce on their ass. I wasn't just responsible for my freedom, but also the freedom of my homies.

I had a few runs to make over on the South Side. I connected with a big homie from Brooklyn, and he was spending major paper. I loved dealing with my up top niggas because they understood the hustle. Not like these Down South lames that didn't wanna work for their shit, but quick to stick another motherfucker up. Trust, I knew I sent a message when I killed those niggas, but in the back of my mind, I knew some fools would try to get at me again. I was ready whenever they're ready to go.

I saw my dude parked in the parking lot over by South Side Plaza, so I pulled up over there. He got out of his truck and got in mines. We chatted for a little, did our business, then parted ways. On my way out of the plaza, I felt like something wasn't right. I had a bad feeling, like I was being watched. I stopped for a second and took a quick glance around, and then pulled off. At this point in the game, I wasn't sure who was after me, the feds or the Creighton niggas. I knew I had no choice but to protect myself by any means necessary.

Luscious, my old Puerto Rican fling, had been blowing me up all day, and truthfully, I needed a break from all the drama and chaos in my life. I was in need of some pussy anyway since I haven't fucked since Sierra got hit. We've decided to meet up at our li'l spot on Midlothian Turnpike. I was ready to tear her walls down, you hear me? As usual, she got there before me and paid for the room. I parked my Range Rover all the way in the back, just to stay out of sight. The last thing I needed was that bitch Mo' to see my shit parked at a fucking motel. I just couldn't deal with all the extra whining.

I called shorty's phone to let her know I was on my way up to her room. I swear my dick got extra hard e'erytime she crossed my mind. I had to admit she was a bad-azz bitch, and she knew how to suck a mean dick. Only problem, she's a ho, and I couldn't turn a ho into a housewife. Straight like that!

As I approached the door, I had that same weird feeling that I had earlier in the day. I felt like someone was watching me again. I turned around, but all I saw was a young mother with her seed standing on the steps, so I shook the feeling off and knocked on the door. I realized the door was ajar so I pushed it open farther and stepped into the room. Shorty was already sprawled out across the bed butt-ass naked. I got supergeeked; I was ready to put some major work in.

"*Hola,* papi." She motioned for me to come over.

"Whaddup, ma? I see you ready to please yo' daddy," I said with a smile.

"Yup, you know me. Your wish is my command."

I quickly undressed and dived on top of the bed. I was ready and able to tear that Puerto Rican pussy up.

I slid the condom on real fast and attempted to spread her legs. Suddenly out of nowhere, I felt a hard object poking me in the back; then I heard a man's voice.

"Boss man, don't move a muscle."

I jumped up and leapt toward the side of the bed, where I had my gun in my jeans pocket. I grabbed it and turned to him. We were now face-to-face, looking dead in each other's eyes. I don't know about ole boy. I was in it to win it, though, and I wasn't going out like that. It was at that very moment that I realized that I was caught slipping in the name of the P-U-S-S-Y.

"Boy, I said don't move. You deaf or something?" This nigga spoke in his deep Southern accent.

"Nah, pussy hole, go suck yuh mumma," I said, pointing my gun straight at him. All along, I was trying to work this scenario out in my head. I only saw one dude, but there could be more hiding, and I was by myself. It wasn't a good look, but I knew I wasn't going down without a fight. I also was trying to figure out if the bitch was in on it. Fuck that. It didn't really matter. She had to go. I don't believe in leaving witnesses behind.

"Empty your pocket, boy."

"My nigga, I ain't emptying shit. You know who I am?" I asked with venom in my voice.

"Nah, homie, I know who you are. The real question is, do you know who *I* am? Better yet, fuck that. I'm big Sanchez from New Orleans. I know you heard them stories about me and my family."

"Oh, that's you, son? Damn, I would never imagine," I lied.

I threw that nigga off by my comment because he started cheesing. I raised my Glock and aimed for his dome. Then I pressed the trigger, letting off about four bullets, back-to-back. The bitch started screaming loud as hell, so I turned my attention to her and finished my clip. Blood was splattering everywhere as her screaming was instantly silenced. I grabbed her cell phone, quickly dressed, and dashed out the door. I ran as fast as I could down the stairs. I was out of bullets. I had to get to my truck so I could reload my gun. I was praying that people hid once they heard the shots. I needed to leave the hotel. I jumped back in my ride, put the gear in reverse, and backed my way out of the parking lot, burning tires all the way up the turnpike. I kept looking in my rearview mirror just to see if anyone was following me. Then I called my boys to meet up at one of my stash houses.

My mind was racing. I was shocked that this bitch tried me like that. I've been dealing with the bitch for a minute and have always blessed her with dough. Oh well, another bitch done tried me, and now her ass done croaked. I would never know who that was or why that bitch chose to cross me, but I knew that my days were numbered!

I got back to the North Side in no time and circled the block a few times before I pulled in the driveway. I got there before the guys, so I called to check on Sierra. Then I called Mom-dukes. I just wanted to hear her warm, gentle voice. We rapped for a minute, then hung up. I needed to take a trip up top so I could spend some quality time with her. She was definitely my queen and my rock.

I washed the blood off my arm and took off the shirt that I wore. Then I lit a blunt and took a few pulls so the strong scent of the herb could fill my nose. All types of thoughts invaded my brain. I couldn't win for losing. I needed to regroup. Who can I trust? Where can I hide?

The fellas finally got to the spot, so it was time for our meeting.

"What a gwann, fellas?" I greeted them, and we exchanged daps.

We all sat in the living room. Chuck brought some Hennessy, so we started to drink and smoke. I had mad love for these dudes, and I knew the feeling was mutual. I went on to tell them about what went down earlier. We sat back like soldiers getting ready to go to war. We were ready for whatever and whoever. It was time to close this chapter of our lives and move on to bigger things. Maybe move farther South. I heard ATL was doing it big. I'll just have to get Sierra to agree.

Chapter Five

Sierra Rogers

I was at home relaxing. I felt much better and decided to do some cooking. I missed cooking for my man. I admit I couldn't cook everything, but my fried chicken was like that, or so he told me. Either way, I loved cooking for him. We really hadn't talked a lot about all the things that happened; instead, we both put our focus on the baby. I loved the fact that he was as excited as me, and outside of being in the streets, I believed he will be a great dad.

I heard the doorbell ring, and everybody knew that I got nervous every time I heard that darn doorbell, so I grabbed my gun. Yes, I still had my .380. I walked over to the door. Shit, it was not who I expected, but I damn sure did not want to see this bitch. I opened the door to see what the hell she wanted.

"What is it? I thought I told you never to show your face around here again."

"Baby, I just need to talk, just five minutes of your time," she pleaded.

"Don't call me baby. My name is Sierra, and I damn sure don't have no time for you. So get tha fuck on before I slam this door in your face," I said in a stern voice and proceeded to close the door. That's when that bitch placed her foot in the door preventing me from closing it. See, this bitch done tried me more than once. I had my gun in my hand, so I pointed it at her head.

"I just told your bitch ass to leave. Don't make me shoot your ass for trespassing."

"Oh my, you would put a gun on yo' mama? I birthed you. I am yo' mama. I just want to talk," she pleaded with tears rolling down her face and her voice trembling.

I don't know what it was, but something that she said struck a nerve in me because I had tears in my eyes too. I was shivering on the inside. I wanted to reach out and hug her, but I was careful not to go that far. I lowered my gun and opened the door.

"Come in. You have five minutes, and after that, I want you gone for good," I warned.

I walked to the kitchen and poured her a glass of lemonade. That's all her ass was getting from me, and even with that, I was being generous. I poured a glass of milk for me and sat on the chair.

"So what's good? After all these years, what the fuck you got to say?"

"Sierra, I know I messed up, and I am so, so sorry. I was on crack real bad, prostituting myself to keep a roof over our head. I was in bad shape; I would not be of any use to you."

"You know what? That's *your* fucking business. I was your child. I needed you. You left me for dead, Mother dearest. At fifteen, you walked out and left your only seed, and now you're here telling me you're sorry? Are you fucking serious?" I blurted out.

She walked over to me and looked in my eyes. "I know it. I was a bad mother. I was selling pussy in the room next to you. I know you done heard some of the noises. I did not deserve you, and you deserved better. I thought that when I left, it would be better for you."

"Better? I had to fuck dope boys to get food, pads, and clothes on my back. I was a ho just to survive, you hear me? I did not choose that life. You handed it to me. I think 'bout that shit all the fucking time."

"That's true, but look at you. You turned out well, and you have a career, a house, a baby on the way, and a man that loves you. I never had that. After my mama died, I was young and pregnant with you, and I had to boost clothes just to buy milk and diapers. Life just got too hard on me, and I turned to crack. I tried to quit, but I couldn't, and before I knew it, I was strung out."

I was not buying her stories. All I could remember was the day that she walked out and how broken I was. Then again, I knew that I was sick of all the tricks that she brought home. I was ready for this conversation to be over, because I was feeling sick all over again.

"Listen, I don't know what you want from me, but I have nothing to give. I am grown now and do not need—and I repeat—do *not* need a mother. I'm happy that you got clean, and you're doing better. But other than that, take your problems to God, ask him for forgiveness, 'cause truthfully, I can't forgive you for what you've done to me. I just can't," I said while shaking my head.

She grabbed my hand and got on her knees. This shit was getting really weird, and I needed to get this woman out of my house fast.

"Sierra, please, I'm begging you. I need you. Please give me another chance. When I heard that you got shot, I burst out crying. I was scared that I would not have a chance to ask for your forgiveness. Now we have a chance to make it right. Please don't take this chance away from me," she pleaded with tears and snot running down her face.

All this shit sounded good, but I could not—would not—allow her back in my life. I just could not go there with her, and I was tired of hearing all the shit. I pushed her hand off of me and stood up.

"Listen, I cannot get over what you did to me, and I am tired of hearing all this crying. You chose to suck on a glass dick; you chose to sell your pussy, so accept that this is the outcome. I will not give you a free pass to walk back in my life. I want you to leave *now!* Please don't come back." I pointed toward the door.

She turned toward me with a look of disbelief plastered on her face. I didn't pay it any mind. Instead, I walked over to the door and opened it. She walked to the door with her head hanging low. When she was completely out the door, I closed it behind her.

I needed a drink. Even though I wasn't supposed to be drinking, I walked over to the kitchen cabinet and poured me a tall glass of Baileys. I took a few huge gulps so I could numb some of the mental pain that I was feeling.

I continued cooking dinner. While the chicken was frying on top of the stove, I walked into the living room and cut the television on. It was

5:00 p.m., and I wanted to catch the news on CBS. The news anchor was reporting a shooting at a motel on the South Side. That motel looked familiar, so I cut the volume up so I could hear what took place.

"I am here reporting from the La Quinta Inn at 3343 Midlothian Turnpike, where officials are reporting a double murder. A young lady and a man were found dead in room 23B. The police are asking for the citizens' help; if you've heard anything, please call the RPD," the reporter said.

I shook my head. I was so tired of all the killing in this city. It even bothered me more, now that I was pregnant. I really need to leave, but those were only fleeting thoughts. I was born and raised here. I couldn't imagine living elsewhere; plus, I had some business to handle.

I finished cooking dinner. Then I made fried potatoes with onions, peppers, fried chicken, and sweet corn. I even made a big glass of lemonade. This was our first official dinner since I've been home.

It was around nine when I heard Alijah open the door. I spoke to him earlier and got a vibe that something was going on with him, but as usual, he didn't really include me in his affairs. I got up and strolled downstairs. I was happy to see my man. After that episode with my egg carrier, I needed a strong shoulder to lean on.

"Hey, babe," I greeted him.

"Hey, ma, how you feeling?" he asked, and then planted a big wet one on my forehead.

"I'm good; your food is on the table. Let me warm it up for you."

"Damn! *That's* what I'm talkin' 'bout. My baby handlin' her business."

"Boy, whatever. Don't I always?" I asked jokingly.

"Nah, it ain't that. I just know you been sick, so I didn't expect this."

"I feel you, but I'm good, though. I haven't been feeling no pain lately, and I was vomiting earlier, but I ate some crackers and drank some ginger ale."

"Yea, my little man is growin'. I can't wait for him to get here."

"Little man? How you so sure? It might be a li'l me."

"Yea, whatever, Sierra, but you better pop out a boy. If not, I'm sending the baby back in there."

"Boy, you trippin'. I can't wait to push. They ain't even got to tell me to push. I'm gonna open my legs wide and make one big-ass push. Trust me, I got this."

"Yea, just don't rip my pussy, 'cause I 'ont want no big pussy gal. You heard!"

We both busted out laughing. That shit sound funny as hell, especially because he spoke in his native tongue. I sat there as he ate and drank a Guinness beer.

"So, ma, you still don't remember anything about the shooting?"

"Baby, no. I'm really trying, you know, but it's like that part of my memory just disappeared."

"OK, cool. No problem. I'm just anxious to know who tha fuck violated you like this."

"I understand, babe, and trust me, I want to know too," I said in a somber tone.

He finished eating, and we headed upstairs. He got in the shower, and I got back in bed. I was going to make love to my man tonight. It's been awhile since I felt his dick, and I was well in need of some good fucking. He got out of the shower, smelling all good. He lay on his back looking at me as if I were a piece of meat, so I winked at him and pulled the towel loose. I could smell the fresh scent of the Irish Spring body wash.

I lay there for a minute so I could savor the moment. I stared at his soft dark manhood, brought my face closer until my lips were touching the tip. I was ready to make sweet love to it. I licked the tip of it a few times, and then licked along the side while working it up and down. It did not take long for it to get hard as a rock. A lot of bitches claimed that they didn't like to suck dick, but I beg to differ. This was my man, and if you left it up to me, I would suck the black off of it. I continued to please him, and I got the feeling that he loved it from his moans and groans.

I wasn't ready to ease up just yet. My intention was to suck him dry, or so I thought because he grabbed my head and pulled it closer to his dick. Regular, round-the-way chicks complained about how their mouth got tired. I was a pro, as sad as it might sound. I'd been sucking dick since I was fifteen years old. I used to use it as a control over weak-ass niggas, but with Alijah, I really enjoyed myself. I felt the veins rising, so I knew he was getting ready to bust.

I started to suck harder and faster, deep throating all nine-and-a-half inches of that Jamaican wood. As he finally exploded in my mouth, I relaxed and let every drop of his milk shake slide down my throat, and when I was finished, I used my tongue to gently clean up every drop that was left. I then got on top of him. I knew I had to get his dick hard once again, so I placed one of my breasts in his mouth. I started to rub his soft dick on my clit, and it rose up instantly. I then slid it into my slippery, tight, sweet jar. I've always loved the feel of his dick as it entered my domain. I slid all the way down on his pole so I could feel the full effect. I bounced on his dick as if I were a professional jockey. The vibe that I was getting was one that I wanted to savor.

He lay there and let me have total control of the situation, that was, until my legs started to tremble. He pulled me closer to him, and I had multiple orgasms. They came on so strong that I felt like the veins in my head were about to bust open, and my body was going into convulsions. I blamed it on the lack of sex. I grabbed on tight to him and released the pressure that I was holding inside. My love juice spilled onto his dick, which must've turned him on because he proceeded to pound on my walls. I start to scream as loud as I could. It was definitely screams of pain and pleasure mixed together. I dug my fingernails into his back as he applied more pressure. After what seemed like forever of an extreme fuck session, he finally busted. I have to admit, the dick was fire, and my pussy was definitely burning up.

I stood up and ran to the bathroom as his come leaked down my legs. Quickly, I jumped into the shower with the biggest smile on my face, thinking, *I love me some him.* He ended up joining me in the shower, and we finished off our sexercise session.

Alijah Jackson

After hanging out with the guys and handling some business, I decided to roll out. It was getting late, and I hated to leave Sierra in the house at night. Even though she has her burner, I still felt the need to be there to protect her, after all that has happened.

My mind was speeding; I was all over the place. First things first, I needed an accountant. I was so used to Markus handling e'erything, but now that he's not here, I have money all over the place. I needed to make a deposit into my accounts, but I was procrastinating because of all the things that had been going on. Shit, I still couldn't come to grips with the fact that holmes was so fucking stupid as to fuck my bitch *and* take my dough, and to make it worse, he never thought that I would figure it out. Oh well, that pussy hole got exactly what he had coming to him. I heard the other day that his family came out here looking for him. His bigmouthed sister even called my phone. I told her ass that dude left without even notifying me. That was my story, and I was sticking to it. I had a talk with Saleem, and he guaranteed me that they will never find his ass, and I was happy because after reading all the evidence that Shayna gave to them pigs,

I wasn't sure that they weren't looking for him *and* looking at me for his disappearance.

The drive home was a long and depressing one. Nothing seemed right to me. I could've lost my life earlier over some pussy. I wasn't sure if anyone saw me leaving or not. I searched my memory to make sure I didn't see anyone on my way out. That's when it hit me that on my way up, there was a woman and a boy in the hallway. I remembered because the boy looked directly in my eyes. I slammed my hand onto the steering wheel.

"Fuck, fuck!"

How did I forget that situation? My blood was boiling. I learned in this game, never to leave any witnesses, and, boy, did I fuck up. I prayed to Jah that they do not connect the dots.

I lit me up a long spliff. I needed my mind right before I entered the house, because Jah knew that I couldn't get Sierra in this mess. How do I even explain to her that I went to cheat on her with the same bitch she fought, and I was set up and ended up killing 'em? That shit didn't even sound right in my mind, so I knew damn well it's not going to sit well with her.

I did my ritual of circling the block before I entered the house. For now, I left all my troubles and the street at the door. I needed to spend some down time with my lady. I knew she been through so much in such a little time since she met me. Sometimes I wonder why she's still around. I mean, I'm a dog. I accepted that, and, yes, I loved all different kinds of pussy. But at the end of the day, I wanted that one special person, and I found her, and now she's having my seed. The next step was to marry her ass, but first, I need a fucking divorce—or hell, nah, I'd be a widower as soon as I find that ole snitching-ass bitch.

This was definitely our first time kicking it like this. She made dinner, and we talked. I wanted us to get back to the point where we hang out and act a fool, but I knew I had to be patient. She was still upset that I went and dug up her moms, but I really thought, and I still believe, that they need to have a relationship.

The night turned out well. I ate, showered, and got some of the best head a man could ever get. Then shorty rode me like I was her stallion, but I loved every moment of it. I wished that I could just stay faithful because she was every man's dream woman. Sexy, independent, and could ride a good dick. Shit, I'd be a fool if I didn't make it official.

Chapter Six

Shayna Jackson

Time flew by, and I was sick and tired of lying low. This was not how I wanted to live my life. I had pictured that by now, I would've been on a beach in South America sipping on a glass of expensive red wine, relaxing with a young buck half my age.

Why is it that Alijah was released from custody and still walking these streets? That's what I was trying to figure out. I've been a defense attorney for years, and I've never seen or heard no shit like that before. It was pure bullshit, especially with all the evidence that I gave them. I knew his money was long, and I wouldn't be surprised if he had the DA in his pockets. I prayed that I was wrong as hell because if that's the case, that would only mean one thing, and that was . . . He knew I set him up. I knew I was thinking all kinds of shit, but I also knew that many times, my intuition was correct. I need to make moves fast and get the hell away from Virginia. Shit, depending on what he knew, I might need to leave the country.

I called Commissioner Sander's office. I had some serious business to discuss with him. He was my only way out of this fucked-up situation. I sure missed Markus, because when he was around, I always knew what was taking place. I still wondered what happened to him. Hopefully, his ass was alive, but I doubt it. Oh well, now was not the time to be worried about the next nigga. I have my own worries, and by the look of things, I was on my own.

The weekend went by fast, and Monday was already upon us. I woke up bright and early, showered, and got dressed in a black Vera Wang pant suit. I had serious business to handle, and I had a feeling it was going to be a long day.

I was out the door by 9:00 a.m. and off to Sanders's office on West Broad Street. I walked in and gave his secretary my name. In no time she motioned for me to go in his office. There he was, sitting behind his wooden desk in a bright yellow suit that resembled a block of welfare cheese.

"Hello, Shayna. I hope it's OK to call you by your first name," he chuckled.

I sat in the chair across from him. He was not even a gentleman. When you see a woman enter your office, you're supposed to stand up and greet her. Not his no-manners-having ass.

"Hello, Commissioner. You can call me whatever the hell you want," I said bluntly.

"What brought you to my neck of the woods? I tried to ring you a few times, but my calls went to voice mail. I thought you kicked me to the curb, and here, you call out of the blue. I tell you, you're one strange lady," he said.

"I'm here on business. Just because I suck and fuck you, that don't mean I want you to blow my fucking phone up," I spat at him.

"Wow! Wow! Hold on, lady, you behaving like I'm just a piece of meat or something."

"Listen, Sanders, this is what I need. I need you to turn over Alijah's file to the feds so they can charge him."

"You know I can't do that. The district attorney's office closed the case because of insufficient evidence. I did my part. I gave them everything that you gave me, and I really thought that we had a strong case, but I guess not."

"Bullshit. I handed you this nigga on a silver platter. I gave you a fucking tape with this man's voice. I gave you all the names of the key players. Damn, what the fuck else did y'all want from me? Fucking blood?"

"Calm down, Ms. Jackson. I fully understand how you feel, but there is nothing further that I can do. You'll just have to sit and wait until he messes up; then we'll get him. I promise you he's on our radar now."

"You bastard! Fuck you. You do not understand how I feel. I risked my life to give this bastard up, and y'all let him slip through the cracks. I have no life because of this. I stay cooped up in a friggin' hotel room. Don't you fucking tell me you know how I feel!"

"I told you, he has no idea that you gave us that information. Your name is protected. I can assure you that you are not involved."

"Assure me? Do you *know* how well connected he is? Shit, he might have this entire department on his payroll. I don't know who to fucking trust."

I stood up and walked toward his window. It was a great view that overlooked Broad Street. I then turned around and walked back toward the desk and looked him dead in the eye.

"I need you to take this case to the feds. Get them on it now!"

"I already told you . . . There is no case. It's closed. Period."

"No, it's not—not as long as you want to keep your fucking job. You know election time is coming up."

"What do you mean?"

"Exactly what I said."

"Pardon my French, but get the fuck out of my office."

"Listen, you fucking bastard, you do as I say, or I will be pressing rape charges against you as soon as I head downstairs."

"Rape? What in God's name are you talkin' about?"

"Hmm. I hope you didn't forget already when you came and paid me a visit in my hotel room and *raped* me," I said sternly while I locked eyes with him.

"You bitch! You came on to me. *You* gave me the pussy. I did *not* rape you!"

"Really? Well, I have the swabs with your semen, I have the tape with me hollering, *begging* you not to hurt me, and I also told you to stop, and to top it off, the hotel has security cameras that I am pretty sure caught you entering my room."

"You dirty bitch! You *gave* me the pussy. I did *not* rape you. *You* came on to *me!*"

"I told you about all the evidence that I have. Correct me if I'm wrong, but in the Great

Commonwealth of Virginia, if a woman says 'stop,' it means stop. Not continue fucking her. With that said, I see a rape charge written all over you."

I could see all the blood drain from his face as he stared at me with his fists balled up. I didn't flinch. I was in control of the situation. I reached in my bag and took out my tape recorder, pressed play, and glanced as he listened to his voice, loud and clear.

"Cut it off, dammit! You evil bitch! You set me up. I should have yo' ass arrested," he stuttered.

I got up and start clapping. "Standing ovation. That was a great performance, Mr. Commissioner, but I think you are not convincing enough. Let's see if you can convince a jury of your peers that you did not rape the vulnerable victim that came to you for help from her killer husband."

I got up to leave. I knew that I had him right where I needed him to be.

"No! Wait! What the hell do you want? Some more dick, money—you name it."

"No. No more of that shit, and I don't want your little chump change. What I *do* want is for you to pursue the case against Alijah. Call up your little fed buddies and get them to open a federal case. I already gave you the evidence; now get me a fucking indictment against him and his crew."

"It's not that fucking easy. I told you that before."

"Make it easy or it will be your black ass sitting in a cell waiting to go to trial. It's your choice."

"Well, lemme see what can be done. Now gi' me that frigging tape." He lunged toward me.

I snatched my hand away. He really thought I was that dumb of a bitch. This was not my only copy. Boy, I tell you how stupid men are. I shook my head in disbelief.

"I wouldn't do that if I were in your position. It could get real ugly up in here," I warned with a deadly look on my face.

"You set me up and now you up in here tryna blackmail me. You are a woman scorned; I cannot believe that I allowed you to weave me in your web of deceit," he said while shaking his head in disbelief.

"Well, Mr. Commissioner, it is called the 'Power of the Pussy.' See, men always think with their cock heads instead of their brains. Don't be too hard on yourself; this has been happening since Adam and Eve's time and will continue to happen. Now, get yourself together. We have work to do."

"Bitch! Get the fuck outta of my office. I will do what I have to do. Other than that, stay the hell away from me, you hear me? Or I will be personally coming for you."

I took my shades off and stepped closer to his face.

"Don't get fooled by this pretty face and tight pussy. Don't come looking for me, especially if I did *not* send for you. I am *that* bitch that your mama warned you about fucking, but I see you didn't listen, ole police boy."

I walked toward the door and opened it. I stepped out in the reception area with my head held high, daring his office slut to say a word. I was done playing with people, and I was out for blood. I felt bad for the next bitch or nigga that crossed my path!

Chapter Seven

Sierra Rogers

My doctor's visit turned out really well. I had a chance to listen to my baby's heartbeat, and on the next visit, I would get to find out what I was having. I've never imagined motherhood to feel this good. I was definitely praying for a girl, but if I get a boy, I'd still be happy. I just pray for a healthy baby. I had no doubt that I'd be a great mom because of what I went through. I made a vow a long time ago that when I had children of my own, I would cherish and protect them until the last breath left my body.

I knew from all my past struggles that I was put on this earth for a reason. I could've died when that bitch shot me, but God had other plans, and I felt like my grandma was watching over me. I couldn't help but wonder if the only time that she becomes visible to me was when I am faced with difficult times. I wasn't going to front; it was a good feeling to know someone was watching over me. I really wished that she had not passed so early; my childhood might've turned out differently. I also heard tons of stories about how sweet she was. I can believe it. I hope she continued to watch over me, because I need an extra set of eyes on me as I embark on this new journey.

I ran some errands and then went home. I had the house to myself for a few days. Alijah was out of town on business. This was my first time being alone by myself, so I kept my gun loaded and close to me. I had been prepared because that bitch caught me slipping once. I couldn't risk another time.

Li'l Mo' was on her way over to hang out with me. It was Friday night, so we were going to smoke some weed, and she was going to drink. This chick was on her way over an hour ago. I always joke with her ass that she was going to be late even for her own damn funeral. I was happy to see her. I've been waiting to taste that sweet flower between her legs. I don't think I'm gay. I do love dick, but I'll have to admit that I love eating Mo's pussy. If a person had told me a year ago that I would be eating pussy, I woulda cussed them out, but like older people always say, "don't knock it, 'til you try it."

I opened the door. My bestie was looking gorgeous in that one-piece Dolce & Gabbana floral jumpsuit. She stayed on point with the latest designer clothes. Can't nobody knock her; baby girl put in major work at the salon. Speaking of salon, I miss being there every day with her. I wanted to return ASAP, but my doctor recommended that I stay on bed rest the remainder of my pregnancy considering I was just recovering from major trauma.

"Hey, Bestie," I greeted her with a huge hug.

"Hey, chick. Sorry that I'm late. I had a late appointment for a full head sew-in. That shit took forever, and then when I did get outta there, I got stuck in traffic coming over. Look like VCU has some type of game going on."

"Mmm. I know you always late, but no worries; the night still young," I said while I winked at her.

We walked to the kitchen. I had to fix her a drink and got me a bottle of water while she prepared to roll the blunt.

"I know, and Lord knows I be trying. Shit, at least, I still show up. Anyway . . . How you and my god-baby doing?"

"They did an ultrasound, and I got to listen to the heartbeat. It sounds strong. Mommy and baby doing good. The only thing is I keep having these headaches, but other than that, I am blessed to be here."

"You right, 'cause I remember when I got the call that you got shot. I almost lost my fucking mind. I did a hundred miles per hour heading to the hospital, but, thank God, you pulled through," she said while shaking her head.

"Yea, I feel you. I still can't believe that bitch shot me, but you know what? I made it, and my baby a'ight."

"Yeah, and your ass need to be resting not running errands. You so hardheaded," she said, giggling.

"I hear you, boo-boo," I joked back.

We moved into the living room and lit the blunt. I went first, and, as usual, she delivered some good weed. I smoked while she smoked and drank. Altogether, we smoked three blunts. To say we were high would be an understatement; we were toasted.

Mo' scooted closer toward me on the couch and started to rub my stomach. The touch of her soft palms sent chills throughout my body. I couldn't find the words to describe the feeling. I pulled her to me and started to kiss her passionately. I enjoyed the smell of her minty breath. We were ready to get it in on the couch when Channel Six Breaking News came on the television. The reporter came on saying there was a shooting at a hotel a few days ago and two people were killed. He also went on to say they had a suspect, and they needed the community's help in identifying this person of interest. We both stopped what we're doing and turned our full attention to the news. I sat there staring at my sixty-inch plasma television. The sketching that they posted looked just like Alijah's face, I looked over at Mo', and I could see that she had the same disbelief look plastered on her face.

"What-the-fuck?" I stuttered.

"Is that Alijah? Oh, hell, nah. It must be a mistake."

If that wasn't bad enough, I almost fainted when they showed the victims' faces; a man and woman. I saw the woman's face and had an instant flashback. The dead bitch was none other than the Puerto Rican broad that I caught him with, the same bitch that I had to beat down. My chest was getting tight, and I was feeling dizzy. I leaned back into the couch as everything around seemed to be spinning. Mo' must've peeped this.

"Sierra, are you feeling a'ight?"

"Not really. I'm dizzy, but I'll be OK. I just need to lie down."

"Do you need me to call an ambulance?"

"No, I'm good. Look in the kitchen cupboard. I have some ginger teabags. Cut the kettle on and boil me some water. I need a cup of tea."

"Sure. I gotcha!"

While she was in the kitchen, I sprawled out on the couch in a daze. *What the fuck this nigga got himself into again?* I just got his ass out of trouble a few months ago. I'd risked my freedom to get his sorry ass out of jail, and here he was again in some shit over pussy that didn't even belong to him. I grabbed my cell that was next to me and dialed his number, but it went straight to voice mail. I hung up.

"I done told his ass about cutting his phone off. What if something's wrong with me or his seed? How am I supposed to reach him? I'm mad as hell right now."

"Sierra, calm down. This is not good for you or the baby."

I just busted out crying. Tears flowed out like a leaky water faucet. All kinds of different thoughts ran through my mind. I couldn't take any more from this nigga. I tried and tried. I done gave him chances. I almost lost my life behind a fucking nigga that ain't even worth it. Mo' hugged me as I wept louder; my heart was broken—yet another time!

I drank the ginger tea and cried some more while Mo' rubbed my back. I eventually dozed off into darkness.

Chapter Eight

Alijah Jackson

This was my first trip up top since Darryl's funeral. So the first stop was his grave. It's been months since I watched them put my brother in the ground, and the pain that I felt was still fresh in my bones, as if he got killed yesterday. I took a seat on top of his grave and thought back on when we first met in the apartment building on Fourth Street. We clicked right away. I was a little younger than him, so I became his little brother. We got deep in the game and promised each other that we'd watch each other's back, and he did; however, I failed him. I admit that I fucked up. Tears filled my eyes, and I tried to hold the grief in. The pain was internal, deep down in my soul. I knelt down on the side of the grave. "Man, I miss you, son. Why you leave me, dawg? We had a fucking deal!" I grieved while hugging his grave.

I saw an older couple that was visiting the grave next to him; they gave me a nasty look. I gritted on their ass and went back minding my own fucking business.

"Bro, I need you. My life is fallin' tha fuck apart. I feel alone, son. God should've taken me instead of you."

I paused; I guess I was waiting on a reply that never came. I just knelt there in silence. Soon, I felt a raindrop, and I thought of a crazy saying back in Jamaica. Whenever it rains, people said that was the dead crying. Shit, I don't usually believe any bullshit like that, but this time, I believe my brother was shedding tears with me. The rain came down in full force on top of me, but I didn't move. My pain was too much to bear. I looked around to see how dark the place had become and decided it was best to leave. I finally got up and dragged my black ass to my truck.

I was soaked, so I drove directly to the crib in the Bronx. I took a quick shower and poured me a glass of Jamaican Overproof Rum; it was just what I needed to cure my heartache. While I was drinking, I thought maybe it was a bad idea to visit the graveside, but I had to let my partna know that I was still around; ain't nothing changed!

Priscilla came through, and we smoked a few blunts and drank some more. I ended up fucking her, and I let that pussy have it. It had been awhile since I fucked anything. I got in about forty-five minutes of long dicking her ass, and then I bust. After that, I got up off her and walked into the bathroom to clean off. In my mind, I was thinking that by the time I got back out there, her ass should be gone. She must've had other plans, 'cause she was sprawled out on the bed.

"Whaddup, B?"

"What you mean?" she replied.

"We fucked, so I figure you was 'bout to bounce up outta here."

"Damn! It's like that? You fuck me and put me out?"

"Nah, it ain't like that, but you already kno' what it is. Ain't nothin' else to rap 'bout."

"Alijah, you know what? Fuck you, nigga. I should've never fucked with yo' ass. If my cousin was here, you wouldn't dare talk to me like this."

"Leave my nigga out of this, and fo' the fuckin' record, I was your cousin's boss, *not* the other way around," I yelled.

"Wow! Mr. High and Fuckin' Mighty. My cousin taught you the motherfucking game, and what'd you do? Your ass got him killed. Yes, Symone told me how it really went down."

"Listen, little girl, stay in yo' fucking lane. I 'ont give a fuck what dat pussyclaat bitch told you. Don't come at me wit' that shit."

"Boy, fuck you. Just the other day, you was chasing this pussy. Now, all because you have a few dollars, you behaving like you the shit. Don't forget where the hell you came from—and plus, yo' dick wasn't all that!"

She got up and grabbed her clothing. I chose not to cuss her young, stupid ass out. Truth was, she was salty wit' a nigga 'cause I didn't want her. It's funny how a bitch could diss you for the next nigga. I remember when I wanted her; she was young, pretty, and had a future. I hollered at her, but she didn't want me then. She literally laughed in my face and told me to get my weight up. I admit the bitch crushed my feelings. So, here I was, years later. My weight was so damn heavy, I'm bring the entire country down, and this bitch think I want her? Fuck, nah! All I wanted was to fuck. Shit, the pussy was not tight; so much for waiting to smash. She finally called a cab and left without saying a word. I downed another glass of rum, smoked another blunt, and fell out in my king-size bed.

***

I woke up the next day with a bad headache. It was no biggie. I had a business meeting with a lot of potential money to make. I was making some major moves, and one of my plans was to take my business back up North. I was killin' it in the South, but after all that happened, I was ready to move back. I love the saying "all money is not good money." So, it was official. I'd stay in Richmond until after Sierra had my seed; then I'm bouncing. I still didn't ask her to move, but I was hoping she would see things my way. I was thinking about moving them to White Plains. It's a very nice place to raise a family; plus, it's out of the way.

Mom-dukes was expecting me, and I was pressed to see her. It'd been a minute since I'd seen her or gotten to hold her and squeeze her tight. I love that woman to death. I can always count on her. From day one, without a father, she held it down, and that's the reason why I would give her my life.

I called her so she could open the door for me, and as usual, we greeted each other with a big hug.

"Mi bwoy, mi glad fi see yuh."

"Mi kno', ma, it's been a minute, but I'm here now."

We sat down on the couch in the living room and started to talk.

"Yuh hungry?"

"Nah. Earlier, I ate two double cheeseburgers."

"A damn cheeseburger? Yuh nyam like di Yankee dem. Dat nuh healthy at all. Yuh is a big man; yuh need real food, cho man."

"Ma, mi gud. Mi wi eat some a your food lata," I said and used my hand to turn her face toward me. I looked in her eyes and noticed how beautiful she was from the first day I laid eyes on her.

"How yuh been?"

"Mi deh yah; mi 'ave life, so mi give tanks to God."

"Of course, dats a must. How's the family?"

"Everybody all right. Mi call dung deh yeseday and everything cool."

"That's what's up."

"So how you do? I haven't seen you since Darryl funeral. Mi kno' how close the two a unuu was."

"I'm livin'. It's been hard, but yuh raise mi fi be tough, so I'm gettin' by."

"So how yuh and Shayna? Yuh wok pon yuh marriage?"

"Mama, mi tell yuh before, we done. Yuh can't even start fi imagine the tings weh she do to mi; trust mi."

"Alijah, y'all were happy before dat young gal cum inna yuh life and mess it up. I don't like dat gal.

I kno' her kind. She's only after yuh money. Mi is a 'oman and mi a tell yuh."

"Ma, Sierra is my woman now, and she's pregnant and ago give yuh your firstborn grand-pickney, so just cool. It's because you don't know the real Shayna why yuh feel like dat still."

I then continued on to tell her everything that went down after I came back from Jamaica. I went into details about my arrest and how I found out that Shayna was behind it. I also told her about Markus and Shayna. I saw the hurt in her eyes as I went on explaining everything in detail.

"Alijah, mi never kno', baby. She fool mi and use mi fi information. A me tell har, you was gone to Jamaica."

"Don't blame yuh self; you couldn't know. She even had me fooled. But don't worry; whenever mi catch her, trust me, she ago pay."

I must've said something that hit a nerve because she scooted closer toward me and grabbed my hands.

"Alijah, baby, listen to mi. Don't hurt that woman; leave it up to God. Trust mi, he will deal wid har—"

"Ma, mi hear yuh, but yuh know, she disrespect me and violate me and mi can't allow that."

"Alijah, yuh is all mi 'ave, and lately, mi feel like yuh is slippin' away. A no suh mi raise yuh, mi raise yuh betta dan this."

I saw the tears rolling down her face, so I used my other hand to wipe them away.

"Stop crying. Yuh kno' you break my heart whenever I see you crying. I wish I could take away your pain, but, Mama, I'm not yuh little baby anymore. I'm grown, and this mi life now."

"Foolishness! Yun nuh learn, yuh friend just dead, and yuh nuh tek heed. You is mi only child, and mi nuh wan' bury yuh."

It broke my heart, hearing her speak like that. I wish I could stop all the pain, but I'd been in the streets since I was a little dude. I lived and breathed the streets, and I couldn't picture my life any other way. I prayed to God that the people close to me would understand the burden they're putting on me. I knew that they only want what's best for me. I know I need to leave the streets now that I had a seed on the way, but I need to do it on my own time.

We ended up talking some more; then we called it a night. I left her some money in the usual spot and kissed her on the forehead. Her eyes were red and swollen from all the crying. I had to bounce; I couldn't take it anymore.

Sierra Rogers

The last few days, Mo' had been staying with me. Alijah wasn't due back in town until the following night. I spoke to him briefly, but I did not mention anything about the incident on the television. I did not trust the phones, even though he changed them on the regular. I couldn't wait until his ass hit the door so I can set it off on him. I had so many questions that I needed answers to real soon. I was sitting there pregnant, and he out getting caught up in a fucking murder of a whore that he claimed he wasn't fucking.

I was grateful that Mo' came over, because if she was not around, I probably would've lost my damn mind up in the house. I wish I could have a drink, but I wouldn't dare take that chance. She cooked me dinner; spaghetti and meatballs, garlic bread and corn bread. This heffa knew how to throw down in the kitchen with her fine ass. I really enjoy being catered to, from breakfast in bed, washed down from head to toe in a bubble bath, to body massage with exotic oils. This was the type of life that I could really get used to, but the fact was, I can't be in a relationship with a woman. It's one thing just to fool around, but to actually be around each other all the time, I can't deal with that. That's too much pussy together. Plus, I love dick and definitely didn't want the fake one either. I loved the feel of hard veins inside of my walls and rubbing against my clit.

Mo' interrupted my thoughts when she entered the room, butt-ass naked, revealing her fat, well-trimmed pussy. I felt an instant tingling between my legs. This was a feeling that I usually get whenever my pussy saw something interesting. I sat there and stared at her as she oiled down her body. I got up and grabbed the bottle of oil out of her hand and poured a small portion in my hand and rubbed both hands together. Then I began rubbing on her breast, gently massaging each of them. I used the other hand to rub between her legs. My fingers strayed into her love hole. It was wet and warm. A sensation invaded my body like no other.

I knelt on my knees so I could dive in it the way I wanted to. I wanted to taste and lick every inch of her body. I started off slowly, started to use my tongue and played with the ring on her clit. I admit that it adds an extra touch of sexiness to her pussy. I inhaled the fresh smell of Dove body wash mixed with the oil that I just rubbed on her. Her pussy was like a magnet pulling my tongue closer, and I just followed the path.

I was so indulged in how well I was pleasing her that I was caught off guard.

"*What the fuck, y'all doing?*" Alijah's voice startled me.

I jumped up in shock! Mo' also jumped to her feet. We both had that nervous looked plastered across our faces.

"Alijah, baby, it is not what it looks like," I stammered.

"What you mean, B? You're on your knees eating out your best friend in our bed. Shit, I'm not mad. I just wanna join in."

"You wanna do *what?*" Mo' questioned him with a smirk on her face.

"You heard me. You over here fuckin' my woman in my bed, so it's only fair I get to fuck both of you."

"Alijah, shut the fuck up wit' yo' disrespectful ass," I spat.

"Watch yo' mouth. All I asked is that since both of you was already eating each other out, lemme give y'all some wood. We all grown."

I walked over to his black ass and smacked him hard.

"Don't you ever—you hear me?—*ever* say that you wanna fuck my friend. Certain shit you just don't say."

He grabbed my arm and shoved me against the wall.

"B, chill out. Don't put your fucking hands on me; don't be showin' off for this bitch."

"Bitch nigga! You done lost yo' mind. The only reason that I'm over here comforting yo' girl is because your ass is incapable of doing it."

"Mo', no disrespect, but call me out of my name again, and I will splatter yo' brains all over your girl's carpet. Make no misunderstanding 'bout it. I said I wanted to fuck you while you was eating my girl. You refused so get yo' shit and get yo' stinking ass out of my crib before I throw you out."

"Nah, hold up. Don't talk to her like that, calling her out of her name and shit." I jumped to her defense.

"Sierra, I caught you with yo' head buried in her pussy. Shit, you still have pussy juice all over your face, so you are in no position to tell me how I need to talk to her ass. You feel me, ma?"

"Boy, please, instead of worrying about whose pussy I was eating, you need to worry about your picture plastered all over the television."

"What? What you talkin' 'bout? I ain't did shit!"

"Really? How did that bitch Luscious that I caught you with end up dead and CBS News has your picture as the prime suspect?"

I could tell that he was shocked. I wasn't sure that he knew about it or was being blamed wrongfully. Either way, I was mad at him.

Mo' got dressed quickly and ran down the stairs. I threw on my robe and chased after her, leaving Alijah sitting on the edge of the bed with his head buried in his palms. I caught up with Mo' before she jumped in her car. I tried to calm her down. I saw the hurt in her eyes, even though she tried to conceal it. I could not blame her for feeling like that; I brought her into the situation. I placed some of the blame on her too, though. She knew that I was in a relationship with him and that did not stop her from getting at me. I really don't condone him talking to her like that, and he was dead-ass wrong for threatening her life. Alijah doesn't know that Mo' has seven big brothers that lived out by Seven Gables Apartments. She was the baby, and make no mistake about it; they'd go to war behind her. I asked her to let it go. She told me yes, but who knows what she was going to do once she got home.

Alijah was sitting on the bed in the dark. I wasn't too sure what he was doing so I stood in the doorway. My gun was on the nightstand, so the chance of me getting to it before him was zero to none.

"What you standin' there fo'?"

"No reason, just tryna figure out why you're sitting in the dark."

"Sierra, cut the bullshit out, B! I'm not gonna hurt you."

"Oh, okay. I don't know; you just snapped earlier."

"Listen, B, I'm pissed the fuck off, but, shit, that's minor. My thing is how long you'd plan on hiding it from me that you're into bitches?"

"First off, I wasn't hiding shit; this is my first time doing that."

"Yeah, right! I been peeped how y'all look at each other, and every time I'd come around, I'd see the dirty looks shorty would give me."

"Alijah, don't even fucking go there. You been playing me from day one. You put me through so much bullshit. Trust me, I'm tired of it all."

"Yo, what the fuck yuh a tal bout? I treat yo' ass good. I'm wit' you. Can't no other bitch call me their man."

"You think you deserve a friggin' trophy? You ain't doing nothing special. I shoulda never fucked with yo' ass after I found out about your wife."

"You stayed 'cause you wanted to. I took you out of the ghetto and turned you into something. So while you wanna be fucking ungrateful, don't you forget *I'm* that nigga!"

I stepped into the room and cut the light on.

"Hold the hell up! Truth be told, I did live in the projects but don't get it twisted. When I met yo' ass, I had my own fucking shit. I didn't ask you for none of this right here. I was going to get it by my-damn-self."

"Whateva, B. You missin' the point, so go ahead with all that. You kno' I 'ont do all that back-and-forth shit."

"Nah, you go the fuck ahead. Let's put it on the fucking table. I've been a fuckin' fool for yo' ass fo' too long. I have been there from the second that I met you. I risked my freedom to get yo' trifling ass out of jail. How the fuck you think you came home? You thought your fucking money brought you home?"

"What you talking 'bout? My lawyer got my case dismissed."

"Really, Alijah? If you really believe that, you dumber than I thought." I laughed while tears rolled down my face.

"So how the fuck I came home, Sierra? What, you fuck the judge?" he asked sarcastically.

"You know what, nigga? Fuck you! Your ass is ungrateful, just like all these other niggas. Only difference is, you are an asshole with money. You know what? I ask myself this same question, and all I can come up with is how stupid I am for loving you."

"Yo, whatever. You with me 'cause this the best dick you ever had. Plus, I got that long money. You can stop faking like you don't know why. Shit, I love yo' ass never like this about no other female, and now you having my seed. You extra special."

"Nigga, save that shit for one of these dumb-ass bitches out there. I'm good. Trust me, you'll see."

"What the fuck you mean by that? Please tell, 'cause you carrying my seed. We in this together. Ain't nobody leaving, believe that."

"You threatening me? You 'ont want to do that. I will go wherever the hell I want to go. I will blow a nigga or bitch brains out if they ever—and I repeat—*ever* try to hurt me or mine."

I stormed out of the room and went downstairs. I made me a cup of hot chocolate and lay back on the couch, trying to calm my temper down. This was not good for my baby.

I stayed on the couch all night. I stayed up most of the time. So many different things were on my mind. My brain was working overtime. As I looked back on my life, just a year ago, I was living on my own in Creighton, and true, it was the projects, but my life was intact. I had a job and roof over my head. It was my dream to leave from there. But looking back, what did

I do? I traded my old life in for this one, and it almost got me killed.

So many unanswered questions up to this day, but the biggest one was . . . How did Shayna get my address? I've only met the bitch twice, and I never gave her my address. The only people that knew where I lay my head at was Alijah, Neisha, and me. I know Alijah and I didn't do it. So, that left only one person, and that was Neisha bitch-ass. I recalled the day she called me and wanted to see me. I also remember when I had to whup her ass. She left upset, and that was the last I heard of her.

There was no way Shayna and Neisha should've crossed paths, but something kept tugging at me. I had to find out who gave that psychotic bitch my address, and I also need to know was it my so-called best friend that gave it to her. "Oh, God!" I yelled out. It was bad enough I already had one bitch to kill. Now, it seemed like I needed to add another one to the list.

I wasn't talking to Alijah, so I pretended like I was asleep when he walked down the stairs. I waited until hearing his car pull off, then jumped up and ran upstairs with my blanket. I picked out a velour jumpsuit, which is about the only thing I could fit in lately and still feel comfortable. I took a quick shower, got dressed, and headed out the door. I got into the car and drove downtown. My final destination was Creighton. I wanted to holler at Charley. I haven't spoken to him lately. The last time I saw him was when I was in the hospital, so I need to hang with him and pick his brain a little.

Driving through my neck of the hood brought back so many memories. Crime was still imminent, but it was still home. Everyone knew each other and looked out for each other. I arrived at the shop and parked in the back. Charley was in the front, parading in front of the mirror as usual.

"Hey, boo, what's up?"

"Look what the wind blow over this side," he joked.

"Give me a hug wit' yo' dramatic ass."

"Of course, hunnty. I missed you."

"I know it. I meant to call you."

"Mmm-hmm. How you feeling? Here sit down, chile. You glowing from the pregnancy."

"Whateva. Fuck how I look. I feel bloated, and I am so ready to drop this load."

"God bless women, 'cause my ass couldn't survive one day, much less nine months like that. Whew-wee," he said while fanning himself.

"Charley, you trippin', but that's why you are a man and not a woman."

"Anyway, sister girl, what's been going on with you and that fine-ass man of yours?"

"Nothing; same old same old. He's happy he's going to be a father."

"I bet he is. Y'all going to spoil that poor child rotten."

"You know it. I can't wait."

"Sierra, what's wrong? I see something bothering you. Gurl, spit it out."

"Boy, I'm good, just a lot . . . You know, getting shot and just able to move around, and this pregnancy. I guess everything is just weighing down on me."

"Well, you a strong woman and a fighter. When I heard you got shot, I rushed up there, but I wasn't allowed to see you. I had no doubt that you'd pull through, though. Did they ever find out who shot you?"

"Nope, not yet. They still looking."

"That is some crazy shit. I don't know whose shoe you stepped on, but they a crazy motherfucker, and even crazier going to Alijah's crib. They must not know about him."

"Yea," I said. I was trying to get off the topic because I didn't want to keep lying about not remembering who shot me.

"So what's going on in your life?"

"You kno' me, gurlll . . . Working as usual. I had to fire Jazmine. Her ass had to go, and she was rude to my clients. You know I can't have no type of shit like that up in here."

"Damn! That's fucked up. Oh well, I ain't like that bitch," I busted out.

"Yes, gurl, after you left, she thought she was the head bitch up in here; that was, until I shut that ass down. You know I don't play no games," he said while clapping his hands.

Charley was not your typical gay dude. He was very flashy and flamboyant and will cuss your ass out in a second. He gets on my nerves sometimes, but I love me some him, and even more since he put his freedom on the line to help me out.

"So, gurl, how is you and Mo' getting along?"

I was drinking a bottle of water and almost spit it out on myself.

"What you mean?"

"Girl, relax. I mean, how the shop going?"

"Everything good so far. We hired a stylist so things wouldn't be so hectic while I'm not there. I'm itching to go back, though, but the doctor told me to wait until after the birth."

"Chile, sit down somewhere. Your man has more than enough money to take care of you and the baby."

"Yea, I love his money, but I love my money more. That way, a nigga won't think I need him. You know what I mean?"

"Hmm . . . Do I sense trouble in paradise? Spill the beans, honey. You know Uncle Charley want to know."

"Ain't nothing to spill. We good." I gave him that look warning him to drop it.

"Charley, when the last time you seen Neisha?"

"Neisha who?"

"Neisha from Creighton that I used to hang with."

"I saw her the other day over by Lucky's store looking a hot mess. I can't believe she on that dope that bad. I stopped to talk to her, and she had a hand full of money looking for Romey. You know she was trying to get some dope. I asked her where she got all that money, and she kept mumbling some off-the-wall shit 'bout she has a rich friend that shower her with money. She wasn't making any sense, so I walked off on her."

"What? A rich friend? She didn't say who it was?"

"Gurl, no, I told you that bitch is strung out. I wouldn't believe anything that came out of her mouth."

"I feel you. I was just curious." Antennas immediately went up in my head. A "rich friend."

Charley was not aware that he just gave me the missing piece of the puzzle. I felt an instant pain in my chest.

"Sierra, you a'ight? You look like you've just seen a ghost."

"No, just a bad feeling and a little pain. I'm just a little tired."

"What you need me to do?"

"Nothing. I'm fine. I just need to head on home. Sorry I can't stay longer," I said.

"Don't worry; go get your rest. I'm going to take you out after you have the baby."

"I would love that, especially after all that I've been through."

"Chile, I almost forgot. Did you see Jeanette?"

"Yea, I seen her, but I don't have anything to say to her. I'm good, trust me."

"Sierra, Sierra, forgive and move on. We all make mistakes; trust me, I know. I wish that I could get one more day with my mother. Just one more day. There's so much I still want to say."

"I feel you, and that's you. I don't want one more second with the bitch. She left me for dead."

I immediately walked out of the shop. I was sick and tired of people coming at me like I was so wrong for not welcoming her with open arms. I know I'm not wrong. She made her bed, so *she* needs to lie in it.

Alijah Jackson

My trip up top worked out well. I just needed to tie up some loose ends in VA. Top of the list was finding Shayna. I had my niggas looking for her, but it seemed like she just vanished. I checked everywhere where she might be and still no sign of her.

The only other thing that I could come up with was that she was in protective custody, and if she was, she might be tucked away somewhere in west bubble fuck. This was how the movies portrayed people who were snitches. The only difference is that this was real life, and I was going to get that bitch one way or another. I put that on my unborn seed.

I was back in the city and was happy to be back home. Sierra and my seed provided that kind of comfort even in the midst of the storm. I knew she wasn't expecting me until tomorrow night. So this was going to be a surprise. I saw her girl's car in the driveway. This was kind of weird because I just spoke to Sierra earlier, and she never mentioned that she was having company.

I didn't like that bitch but kept my cool because of the friendship that she has with Sierra. I was even was more suspicious after Sierra got shot. In my eyes, everybody was a suspect until I could prove different.

The downstairs lights were turned off, so I made my way upstairs. I see Sierra wasn't on her game because the alarm wasn't set, and she didn't hear me enter the house. I entered the bedroom and in front of me was every man's wildest dream. My woman was on her knees eating out her best friend. I stood there taking in the scenery. I was at a loss for words. I mean, I'm no stranger to this type of shit. I was only shocked that Sierra got down like that. Damn! All this time we could've been sharing bitches.

I cleared my throat and let them know I was standing there. Sierra jumped to her feet and looked at me. I was not tight; instead, I was pleased to see two sexy, fat-ass females in front of me. I told Sierra my intentions, and she felt like I was dissing her. She behaved just like a woman. She got caught and now wanted to scream foul. I decided it was a waste of my time because they were not trying to let me smash. I told her girl to get the fuck out of my crib, and that triggered that bitch to come at me sideways. I had to stop myself from shooting her ass dead.

Her mouth was lethal, and that was the reason why I didn't fuck bitches from the projects. They believe they can talk to a nigga any old way, but where they fucked up at is not knowing I was a different type of nigga. I will drop a bitch quick. Sierra really caught me off guard when she mentioned that my picture was on the news—as if things could get any worse. I was really hoping that I had a clean getaway from that scene, but the face of that little nigga lingered in my mind.

Sierra's girl left, and she followed after her. I put my head in my palms. I was stressed the fuck out. The game had definitely changed, and I had to act fast. Playtime was over. I had to shut shop down. I made me a glass of Henney and waited on Sierra to come inside. I was ready to lay everything out on the table. It was either now or never!

Shayna Jackson

It's been awhile since I spoke to my parents, so I called and had a long talk with Daddy. Times like these, I wished that I was back home with him. However, I was a big girl and could handle whatever situation that came my way. I bet he'd be proud of me if I told him how I stood my ground against Alijah. I didn't want to alarm him, so I decided not to tell him about all the chaos that was taking place in my life.

I got a phone call from Sanders early Friday morning.

"Hello, Sanders, I hope you have some good news for me."

"Be in my office Monday at 9:00 a.m. sharp," he said angrily and hung up before I could get one word in.

"That's rude," I said to myself.

He really needed to brighten up a little. I shook my head and thought the nerve of some men. That phone call meant something important. I did not know what it was, but I just know it moistened my pussy. I got up and took out Mr. Mandingo. That was the name of my twelve-inch pearl dildo. This had been my only source of company as of lately. I can honestly say that I really enjoyed fucking myself because I don't have to worry about sucking it to get an erection, and we can go at it all night long. Hmm . . . Whoever made him was one brilliant sucker.

I poured a glass of my California Zinfandel wine and took out my K-Y Jelly. My pussy stayed wet, but I still love to moisten up Mr. Mandingo a little. After sipping on the wine, I started to get a sensational tingling. I gently squeezed and stroked my partner, then slid him into my high-maintenance pussy hole. The gentle ripples on the dildo shaft provided me with additional stimulation. I grabbed the hollow balls and thrusted deeper in. My body trembled, and I was forced into multiple orgasms. I continued on into hours of pleasure until I finally ran out of come. I fell out in the bed which was soaked with pussy juice. I let the dildo remain inside me as I dozed off into the night.

It was ten minutes to nine when I pranced my black tail to the commissioner's office. I was dressed in a red Anne Klein pantsuit with a pair of pumps. I had my hair pinned up in a bun and little makeup on. I've learned first appearance was always the most important one. I had to be on point since I was not sure what I was walking into.

The office slut was present as usual, so I gave her my name as she looked at me with envy in her eyes. I knew deep down that simple bitch wished she looked as good as me. She told me the commissioner was waiting for me. I pushed the door to his office; I was ready to show my ass if this was some stupid meeting. That thought quickly diminished when I realized that there were three others in the room. I could see "feds" written all over them.

"Hello, Mrs. Jackson, take a seat. These are Agents Duhaney, Swasburg, and the beautiful Agent Rozzario," Sanders said.

"Hello, nice to meet you all," I said.

"Well, the purpose of this meeting is to discuss our mutual person of interest: your husband, Alijah Jackson."

"Really, what is this meeting about?"

I wondered if I should have brought my lawyer along with me.

"Have a seat; we might be here for a while," Agent Duhaney instructed.

Agent Rozzario got up out of her seat and walked around to my side of the table.

"Okay, we are all here, so I will start. This is the bottom line. We have been on to your husband's trail since he first stepped foot in the Commonwealth. One of our undercover agents gave us his name. We do know about his crimes."

"So why he is not locked up then, and why are you telling me this?"

"Sanders came to us last week with evidence that you gave his office, and after going through each piece with a fine-tooth comb, I think we can finally nail him for all the drugs and murders.

We have also brought in Agent Swasburg from the New York Division of the FBI. I believe it's time that we put your husband and his crew away for life."

"All right, you have all this. I ask you again, why am *I* here?"

"You're here because you are married to him. You know him better than any one of us."

"I get that, but I already did my part. I gave y'all everything, including him admitting to his crimes on tape. Richmond police fucked it up and let him walk. I am not doing this anymore; y'all have to do this on your own."

I got up out of my chair; I was ready to leave. This smart-ass bitch walked in front of me and blocked my path.

"Shayna, sit down! This meeting is far from over. I'm going to take this case to the federal grand jury, and I want you to testify."

I did not sit down. This bitch had me twisted, talking to me like that.

"I'm not testifying. I gave you all the evidence. Get the indictment from that. In case you were not aware, Rozzario, I'm a defense attorney, so I know the law. I am still legally married to Alijah, so I cannot be forced to testify against my spouse. I believe that is spousal privilege . . . Yes, that's what it is." I looked her dead in the eyes.

Then I looked at Sanders, and his face was
gleaming. I knew the bastard was enjoying every
bit of this masquerade. I shot him a dirty look.

"Well, Mrs. Jackson, since you are familiar
with the law, you should be aware of what I
am about to say. I am going to charge you with
conspiracy to commit murder, drug trafficking,
money laundering, and last, but not least, the
attempted murder of Mr. Jackson's live-in girl-
friend and the mother of his unborn child."

I froze in the spot that I was standing. I wondered if I heard this Spanish bitch correctly.
How did she know that I shot Sierra? Slowly I
took a seat and tried to regroup quickly. I heard
Sanders chuckling. I wanted to shut his faggot
ass up, but I was in no position to do that. The
truth was, I was just served with a severe case of
reality.

"Mrs. Jackson, let's stop fucking around. Your
hands are just as dirty as those of your husband;
however, I have no interest in you. I am prepared to offer full immunity in exchange for your
testimony—in front of the grand jury and at his
trial. I am also offering the witness protection
program with a new identity."

"You think you have it all figured out for my
life? Y'all some dirty bastards. I came to you
guys for help, and *this* is how I get treated?
Really?"

"Cut out the performance. There's a cell with a cot waiting on you. The decision is yours to make. You have forty-eight hours to get back to us, and, oh yea, we know all about you fucking Sanders, and then trying to blackmail him. See, honey, while you was busy setting him up, he was one step ahead of you. We have everything on video. I have to admit, you are one slick woman," Agent Rozzario said.

I wanted to leap over the desk and put my tiny little fingers around his neck, cutting off his air, and then watch him die slowly. Instead, I got up out of the chair and opened the door and walked out without saying a word.

I couldn't say I was shocked. I was *pissed* because I tried to help these fuckers, and they turned around and fucked me as if *I* was a common whore. The secretary slut had a smile on her face as if she knew what just went down in the office. I still held my head high and hurriedly walked past her. I needed to get a strong drink and regroup. That federal bitch thought she was the shit, but she needed to know, there's only one of me—and I was the *head bitch!*

Chapter Nine

Alijah Jackson

I called a meeting ASAP after learning that I was a suspect in the murders. I wasn't sure who saw it, so I could not risk getting picked up. I need to get out of VA like yesterday. At this point, I did not know who I could trust anymore except my crew.

We decided to meet in the parking lot by Virginia Center Commons. I tried to be extra careful since I wasn't sure that I wasn't under surveillance. Chuck, Dre, and Damion were present. Damion was the newest addition to the crew. He was supposed to be helping me stretch my network out to the Carolinas, but from the look of things, that might not even pop off. We dapped each other up and wasted no time with small talk. I knew my time was limited, and my back was against the wall.

"I called this meeting 'cause a situation presented itself, and I popped off a few days ago. I was made aware that there's an eyewitness, so with that said, it's time to leave this place."

"What type of situation and where?" Damion asked.

"Brethren, this not something that I'm about to discuss. It was personal, I handled it, and that's that!" I snapped.

"A'ight, boss man, how soon you talkin' 'bout?" Chuck questioned.

"Well, that's why I wanted to rap wit' y'all. How fast can y'all get rid of the work we have?"

"Shit, I say, 'bout two weeks, at the earliest."

"A'ight, make it happen. We cleaning house. Shut e'erything down in two weeks, then we out."

"So, what you plan on doing 'bout your situation?"

"I ain't goin' do shit. I'm 'bout to bounce up outta here, move the fuck on to bigger and better things. You feel me?"

"Gotcha, boss man!"

This new pussy hole was definitely getting on my nerves. He was questioning me like I was a bitch or something.

"Son, you already know it's whatever. You roll, and *we* roll," Dre chimed in.

"No question. Let's get it done."

I was about to jump in the truck when I remembered something.

"One more thing, this was a private meeting."

They all nodded yes, and I jumped in the truck and sped off. I didn't get too far down the block when I noticed a black SUV following closely behind me. It caught my attention because it pulled out right after I exited the mall parking lot. I knew that I was semiparanoid, but I couldn't take any chances. I took some different turns, then pulled over at the Texaco on Laburnum Avenue. I watched as it sped past. I tried to get a glimpse of who was driving, but the windows were tinted jet black.

I took a detour, and instead of heading home, I headed to Fairfield. I called Saleem so he'd know I was on my way to see him. I needed to rap with him real quick; plus, it'd been a minute since we kicked it. I drove around the back side of the building. I knocked a few times, and he opened the back door.

"Whaddup, son?"

"Peace my brother."

"Pour me a strong drink."

"Gotcha!"

He poured two drinks, and we sat down. The store was closed for the day, so we were by ourselves.

"How did your trip up top turn out?"

"E'erything cultured. You know me. If it ain't no dollars involved, I'm not fucking with it," I bragged.

"Understand."

"Bro, I want to holla at you 'bout some real shit. I think them pigs are after me about a double murder that happened the other day."

"What the fuck? How?"

"Man, I fucked up. I was trying to fuck the Puerto Rican bitch and went to see her in a motel on Midlothian Turnpike, and when I got there, a dude stuck me up. I ain't had no choice but to kill both of them."

"How the fuck they traced it back to you?"

"On my way up, I passed a woman with a li'l homie, and he looked me dead in my eyes as I walked by. That's the only way possible."

"Damn, brother! How you know the pigs looking for you?"

"Sierra saw the news the other night, and they had a sketch of my face. They also offering a reward."

"Yea, that doesn't sound good at all. You need to bounce ASAP."

"I know that. The timing is off, though."

"I know this ain't the right time to put this on you, but I have no choice. I found out who was responsible for shooting Sierra. See, I had my connect put out a bounty on the person head, and sure enough, the streets start talking."

"Bro, cut all the unnecessary info. Who did it?"

"Word is, it's your wife."

"Wha the bumboclaat yuh a sey?"

"My connect is legit; haven't failed me as yet."

"Yo, bro, this bitch is out to get me. How the fuck? I was so fucking blind. This bitch was out to get me all along."

"Brother Man, we had the conversation a few months back, and I told you to handle the situation that you had with her. She's a scorned woman that will do anything to get your attention."

"I'm hearing you, son, but we talkin' 'bout the bitch that I married. I gave the world to her."

"True, you gave her everything, *except* you. A woman like Shayna is not to be taken for granted. I warned you about this."

"You did, and I didn't listen. This bitch played me, and now she violated me. This leaves me no choice but to hunt her down and put her out of her misery."

"Shit, if she's working for the law, only Allah knows where she's at right now. Be very careful; you might just walk into a trap."

"I feel you on that. Another thing, I'm closing up shop, getting out of here. Shit ain't right. At times, I feel like I'm being followed, and I don't know how much Shayna know. I can't linger around."

"Wise choice, my brother."

He grabbed my arm, and then he spoke. "Listen to your inner gut. Trust no one, and I mean, *no one*. You are a man destined for greatness, but too many Jinns is in the way. Leave, start over. I will always be here if you need to reach me."

"I know, bro. You always have my back, and I love you for that. You know I will lay a nigga or an entire family down for you. We ain't blood, but loyalty has bound us together."

"Brother, we love the game, but these streets are mean and cruel. I lost my li'l brother to the streets, and each day I realize this ain't the life, but this is all I know. You're still young, and you have a family. Get out and live your life."

"Yea, bro, I think 'bout it e'eryday. I want to be around to raise my seed. I didn't have no pops so Mom-dukes held it down as much as she could, but the fact is, these streets raised me. I want different for my seed."

"That's a decision only you can make; you know that. Only a few of us ever made it out.

Either you're six feet under or pressing a bunk in prison."

"Well, I can't risk either, so I'm about to be ghost in exactly two weeks."

"Sounds good; be easy. Be your own guardian. Protect yourself, my brother."

"A'ight, son."

He let me out the door, and we dapped each other; then I got into my truck. This talk between us was so tense. I love rapping with him because whenever we do, I always walk away with some type of knowledge.

I headed home to holla at Sierra about the move I was ready to make. I needed to know what it was—either she was riding with me or not. I would prefer if she did, 'cause I need to be in my child's life. I felt like I was ready to settle down with her and be a family. I didn't want to lose her behind some fuckery.

On the drive home, I probed my memory to remember all the places that Shayna talked about visiting, all the different states that we visited together. I knew that she didn't fall off the face of the earth. Somebody, somewhere know where the fuck she's at. I need to turn the heat up, and I bet you motherfuckers will start talking.

Chapter Ten

Sierra Rogers

So much had been going on. Alijah and I barely spoke to each other. I sent him a message that I was sick of him and his bullshit. I knew I was a good bitch and plenty niggas would love to wife me. If he continued playing his childish-ass games, he'd find himself alone.

I've been a hustler from the time I was a child, so taking care of me was no big deal. I was tempted to walk away from the house and go find me a two-bedroom apartment. I wasn't one of these dumb bitches that needed a fucking man. I looked at it like this . . . I could do for myself, and I please myself if I have to. Don't get me wrong, I loved him and wanted a family with him, but I wouldn't deal with no disrespectful-ass dude that thought because his money was long, he could disrespect me. I knew my pussy was tight and wet. I could ride a dick, had a cute face, and had a career. So niggas better come correct.

Li'l Mo' was still in her feelings; honestly, I didn't understand the reason behind it. She knew I had a man, yet she had the nerve to ask me to leave him. That was some crazy shit right there. I liked pussy; might can go a little further and say I loved pussy, but I would not be in any type of relationship with another woman. Bitches were needy, had too many hormones. That was too much pussy rubbing together and not enough dicks in between. I had to shut her down. I loved her as a friend, and I had a physical attraction to her, but I loved my man more and was not going to leave him for her. I really hoped she understood where I was coming from and let it go so we can remain friends.

Jeanette had been on my mind a lot lately. I don't know why because I still had no understanding of how she up and left her only child. She left me around drug addicts, murderers, and rapists. I wondered if I ever crossed her mind the entire time that she was gone. At first, I didn't want to talk to her, but over the weeks, it's been bothering me. I needed answers, and the only person that could give them to me was my egg donor.

I recalled that the last time she was here. She left her address and phone number. I was going to throw it away, but something held me back. I left it on the coffee table in the living room. I decided to get it and pay her a visit. The day was cold and brisk, but I wasn't going to let it sway me away from going around Whitcomb Courts. I needed to see her.

I pulled up on Whitcomb Street, then double-checked the address she wrote on the paper. I found the address and parked my car. I hopped my pregnant tail to the door. I didn't like to come to Whitcomb because these dudes were not nice, and they stay beefing with Creighton niggas. They had a reputation for jumping people. If you get into a fight with one, you can expect the whole family, including the grandma, to jump on you.

I banged on the iron door. There was no response. I banged a few more times, waited a few seconds, then decided to leave. Suddenly, the door popped open, and I turned around. She stared at me as if I were a ghost.

"W-h-a-t are you doing here?"

"Hello, Jeanette. I didn't think I needed an invitation."

"No, no, baby, just never thought you would come. Here, come in and have a seat."

Against my better judgment, I followed her inside, and the first thing that caught my nosy ass was the scent of stale urine. The carpet was torn up, dirty, and covered with Kool-Aid stains. There was no furniture; a white plastic chair was by the doorway. I wasn't going to sit down, especially after I just saw about three roaches crawling along the wall by the door. I felt nauseated. The bagel and egg sandwich I ate earlier were getting ready to come right back up.

I needed air. I had to step outside.

"Look, let's step outside. I can't breathe up in here." I opened the door and walked outside and immediately welcomed the cold air that hit my face. She also stepped outside.

"You know, you shouldn't be in the cold like this. You're pregnant, plus your health is not at its best."

"Listen, I got this! Whose apartment is this? It's filthy."

"It's a friend of mine. I help out with the chirren, and she gives me a place to lay my head."

"No children should live in such filth, and you ain't no better living like that."

"Sierra, I don't think you came all the way from the West End to interrogate me about how I'm living."

"You are so right. Excuse me if I overstepped my boundaries," I replied sarcastically.

"OK, why are you here? A few weeks ago, you threw me out of your mansion and told me you never wanted to see me again. Now you pop up, turning your nose up at the only place that I have to lay my head."

"I see ain't nothing changed. You are still being defensive, like I am supposed to accept you with open arms."

"Chile, you a grown woman, so do what you please. If you're here to tell me how horrible of a parent I am or how much you hate me, I really don't want to hear it. I admit I fucked up, but bashing me is not going to change a damn thing."

"That's funny! I didn't come here to bash you or to get your pity. I thought you were dead and to my astonishment, you were not, and you just walked into my life. I have a lot of questions, and I need answers."

"I can give you all the answers that you seek, but what good is it going to do? You will only find more reasons to hate me."

"You think you know me? You have it all figured out, right? You have *no* idea about me or my feelings."

"It's cold, and I do not own a jacket. I can't stand out here going back and forth."

"I'm not going anywhere until you explain to me why you chose a glass dick over me. Also, who is my father? And I have tons of other questions. You can get in my car, and we can go eat lunch at the little seafood spot in Mechanicsville."

I got in the car and cut the heat on. Damn, it was cold. I never understood why Virginia gets so cold. I need to move to Arizona or one of those states that stay hot all year-round. I waited as Jeanette locked up the apartment, pranced toward my car, opened the door, and got in.

"This is a real nice ride."

"Mmm-hmm."

"That fella Alijah really takes good care of you. I think you have a keeper on your hands."

"Jeanette, you don't know anything about my life, so please don't speak on it. That's me and my man's business what he does for me."

"Excuse me, I just thought—"

"Well, you thought wrong. Let's just stay on the topic of child abandonment. *That's* what I want to discuss."

I drove to Ken's Seafood and got us a table. It was strange sitting across from the woman that gave me life; the same woman that I hated all these years. As we waited to get served, I glanced at her face. I saw that she had aged a lot, but her skin was clear, and she looked cleaner than the last time that I saw her when she had abandoned me. Back then, she was dingy looking. Her hair was matted, and she had track marks all over her arms. I wasn't sure what made her change, but I was ready to dig into the life of a certified crackhead.

The waiter brought our food, and I watched as she dug into the seafood platter I'd ordered for her.

"Excuse my manners. I should've waited on you."

"No, go right ahead. Enjoy your meal."

We ate, drank, and then started to talk. Well, I was asking the questions. I admit that I was harsh at times, but it didn't bother me any. I was the only victim here, and I was not going to ease up. We went back and forth for a while. It even got so tense that we both started crying. I wept hard. I had years of emotions bottled up inside of me and needed to let it out. I needed a mother to teach me the little girl things. I needed her love.

She startled me when she moved to my side of the table and wrapped her arms around me.

"Baby, I am so sorry for leaving you. I can't change the past, but please give me a chance to be in you and my grandbaby's life."

"I'm scared, Mama," I mumbled.

"I know you are, baby, but we can try together."

I swear that I didn't like the way I was feeling. I was in a vulnerable state. I felt like that fifteen-year-old little girl that needed her mommy. My heart was hurting and was telling me the total opposite of what my mind was saying. My mind was telling me not to trust her, but my heart was crying out for a mother's love.

People in the restaurant walked by and stared at us. I paid them no mind because they had no idea what I have gone through. I eventually got my crying under control and continued asking questions. She answered most of them, even though some of the answers were bull-shit. I couldn't really blame a crackhead for not remembering. I heard stories that drugs burn the brain cells out.

I paid the waitress, and we left without me touching much of my food.

"I really enjoyed lunch. You have no idea how much this means to me."

"No worries. I needed answers, and I got most of them. Maybe I can finally sleep."

I drove her back to Whitcomb, but when I pulled up, I got this feeling like I was not going to see her again. That's when I decided to make the craziest decision ever.

"You know, you can stay with us until you get on your feet."

"No, I couldn't do that. Y'all need the space."

"I got space. Just looking at this dump you're living in makes my stomach turn. It's your life, though, so it's your decision."

"OK, give me a few days so I can decide what I want to do. Plus, I would have to give the chile notice so she can find another babysitter. I can't just leave her hanging like that."

"All right, it's your life. Put my number in your phone and call me if you decide to come."

She exited the car, and I drove off. I needed to rest. I felt mentally and physically drained. This baby was just draining my energy. Only God knows how ready I was to drop this load, I thought as I rubbed my stomach.

Alijah wasn't home, so I had some time by myself. I took a hot shower and got dressed in a pair of pajamas. I needed to lie down; I had heartburn, and it was killing me. I popped me some TUMS and crawled under my comforter. I had a lot on my mind. I wasn't sure that I made the best decision earlier. I really did not know this woman. I wasn't even sure if she wasn't still doing drugs. I've been around crackheads enough to know that they will lie their ass off about not getting high. I whispered a prayer to God to take the wheel. If she ever decided to move in and I found out that she's still getting high or still selling pussy for a hit, I was going for her head. I do not want that around my baby. Point-blank, period!

I was in a deep sleep when I felt someone shaking me. I jumped up without hesitation. My first instinct was to grab my gun that was underneath my pillow. I realized it was Alijah when I opened my eyes. I sat up in bed staring at him. I wanted to ask him what the hell he woke me up for, but I refrained from doing so because of his disheveled appearance. His hair was a hot mess, I guess because I haven't been braiding it. His clothes were not ironed, and he looked like he'd aged about ten years.

"What's going on? You all right?"

"I'm good. I need to holla at you."

"I'm tired. This can't wait until morning?"

"No, it can't. We need to talk now!" he said in his mean-ass voice.

I rolled my eyes and thought, *Here we go again*. I sat there looking at him, like, nigga, speak already.

"Yo, B, I know I fucked up, but I'm human, and it was never my intention to hurt you."

"Alijah, we've been down this road before many times, and I keep telling you, I don't want to go through this shit anymore. You lied to me 'bout fucking that slut, and now you wanted for her murder. You fucked up your life over a nasty piece of pussy when you have good pussy at home."

"Sierra, it ain't even about that. I fucked up, yo, but that's the past. I need to know that you still wit' me; that you still have my back."

"Why does it matter now? Is it because you need me now?"

"Slow your roll. I 'ont need a motherfucka except God. Him alone mi need. Is yuh mi need and want inna mi life."

"Alijah, I been here. You just didn't care. You were too busy fucking them other bitches, and see what it got you? One bitch set you up, and the other bitch served you with a murder charge."

"I hear you, but fuck that. Right now, don't none that matter. I'm leaving in two weeks, and I want to take you with me."

"You're leaving? So when did you come up with this decision?"

"I've been thinking about it lately. I need to bounce. I'm hot right now. I know it's only a matter of time before they put my name to that sketch. The nigga that I popped is from a clique in New Orleans, so either way, I'm a wanted man."

"Now you want to drag me and my baby into your world of madness? *You* chose this life, I didn't. I was only looking for love and a way out of the projects."

"Listen, you knew what kind of life you were getting into, so get the fuck outta here with all this holy shit you spittin'. You can sit here running your mouth, but at the end of the fucking day, is either you riding with me or you're not. There's no in between."

Tears poured down my face. I recalled growing up; all I ever wanted was a way out of poverty. I admit I made some fucked-up choices too, but I didn't want all this chaos in my life.

"I fucking love you, but I want more than just us playing house and you running the streets. I lay up in here sometimes lonely, and days pass before I see your face. I worry myself every time that you walk out the door, anytime the phone rings late at night. I get a sick feeling in my stomach. This ain't no life for me or my baby."

"I'm trying to give you that life. Believe me, I am, but I can't remain in Richmond. If them pigs get ahold of me, I'll be gone for life. My hands are dirty, and these muthafuckas ain't going stop 'til they get me."

I saw the seriousness of what he was saying, and I knew shit just got real.

"Alijah, I can't leave right now. My life is in Richmond. I took your advice and had a talk with Jeanette. I even asked her to move in here until she gets on her feet."

"A'ight, that's cool and all, but right now, all I give a fuck about is you and my seed. What life you have out here? Just months ago, all you had was me; now, out of the blue, you have a life?"

"See? You'll never get it, and that's fine. I just want to stay and have my baby; then we'll come after that."

"What the fuck you saying? I'm not going to see my seed being born?" he yelled.

"You need to calm down. You know I have a high-risk pregnancy, and you still expect me to travel with you to God knows where? I told your hardheaded ass that we'll come after."

"Cool. Your decision," he said before he stormed out of the room.

I lay back down wondering when it would end. I was torn. I wanted to leave with him, but I wanted to have my baby first; plus, I had my own issues to deal with. I decided to stay, have my baby, then turn up the heat on these bitches and show them how wicked I could get!

Shayna Jackson

Forty-eight hours came and went by real quick. I was ready to get on the stand to testify against Alijah. I didn't like how they played me. I felt like they fucked me in the ass without lubricant, and I was livid.

I thought we were all on the same team. They wanted him bad, and I wanted him gone for good. I figured his cocky ass thought that because the charges were dropped, he was the shit. Little did he know but his address was getting ready to change. Hmm . . . I really hope that when they get him, he will shoot at them so they can return fire and kill his black ass. That way, I won't have to worry about divorcing his ass.

Daddy called and told me that Alijah was searching for me. We had nothing to discuss, and furthermore, I can't trust that he's not aware that I set him up. Fuck my husband! All our dealings were over for good!

It was Wednesday morning, and at 9:00 a.m. sharp, I walked into the federal building. My lawyer was going to meet me there. I was a lawyer myself and was familiar with the federal government, but I decided I needed to get a lawyer to cover my behind. I hired Benjamin Kraffe, a well-known defense attorney that was a former prosecutor. I did a little research on him. I had to know he'd protect me by any means necessary.

The feds were present along with that faggot Sanders. I still can't come to grasps that I allowed him to fuck me and still got caught up in *his* plot. I was so tempted to show that bastard that I was not to be fucked with. I knew that would not be a good move on my part, however; killing a cop in the state of Virginia would definitely carry the electric chair.

It was showtime, and it was my turn to get on the stand. The special prosecutor was a young blonde that seemed like she was hungry to get this case going. I don't know her, but I know she had the same intention as I did. I was sworn under oath to tell the truth and nothing but the truth. I was drilled on the stand for an hour and a half: drug deals, murders, money laundering, friends, and associates. Every inch of Alijah's life from the time I met him was under the microscope. It was my pleasure to inform them of everything I witnessed, heard from Markus, or just made up. I even dropped a few tears to make sure his fate was sealed and delivered the right way!

I was excused, and I felt relieved. I was tired of hiding and needed to know that he would be locked up far away. I spoke with my lawyer who assured me that everything on my end was good. I shook his hand and quickly left the courthouse. I needed to get the fuck away from there fast. There was just something about the feds that made my skin crawl.

I've had a nagging feeling about the crackhead that something wasn't right. I wondered how the feds knew that I shot Alijah's ho. I wanted to ask them that but decided to leave it alone. I still had the crackhead's number somewhere, so I searched for it. I wanna know if that bitch was running her mouth, or was it Sierra that gave them my name. I should've killed her, though I thought I did. I didn't have enough time to check and make sure she was dead at the time.

I made the call and left to meet up with the crackhead. My skin crawled every time that I got close to her. The scent alone was killing me. I don't know how in God's name she can't smell that stinky, rotten pussy begging for soap and water. Just the mere thought of that scent turned my stomach. I decide to change the spot we usually meet up at. I couldn't trust her ass and didn't want to chance being seen with her. I couldn't put my trust in another bitch, let alone a crackhead.

I got there ahead of time so I could make a quick surveillance of my surroundings. I watched as she drove up in that same old car that seemed like the engine was about to drop out any second. She saw me and pulled up beside me. I placed a large plastic bag on the seat that I had just for this occasion. This was the kind of smell that might never go away.

She opened my car and peeked her head in.

"Get in and sit down," I motioned.

"What for? I thought the last time you told me that you never wanted to see my face again."

"Sit down and shut up. You're letting my heat out of the car."

This bitch was working my nerves. I just wanted to bust her in the head.

"All right, all right, you the boss," she said before placing her stanking ass on the plastic.

"Good! Let me ask you, did the police ever question you about knowing me or about anything else?" I stared dead in that ho's eyes to see if I could catch any hint of deception.

"Nah, I ain't talk to no cops. I-I don't want to get mix up with no police."

"If you keep your mouth shut, then you don't have anything to worry about."

"Hmm . . . I think *you* have a problem. There was this one guy that came around the way offering a million dollars for information about who shot Sierra. See, I know it was you. That's why you didn't want me to tell anyone that I gave you that address," she said, giggling.

"Listen to me, you little crackhead bitch. You better keep your mouth shut. You hear me?— before they find *you* at the bottom of the James River!" I snapped.

"Look at you. You are scared I'ma say something. Don't worry; your little secret is safe with me . . . that's, of course, if you give me a hundred grand."

"Huh? Bitch, you done lost your mind. Why in this fucking life do you think that I would give your raggedy ass a hundred grand? Bitch, I would *kill* your ass before I did that."

"Ha-ha. You couldn't even kill the person that took your husband from you, so, please, lady, don't bring that shit to me. Don't be fooled by my looks. I was born and raised in Creighton Court Projects, and I know how to fuck up a bitch. Believe that!"

"Just pathetic. I'm giving you one last chance to get your bitch ass out of my car. You hear me—before I blow your fucking brains out."

I was contemplating on getting my gun out of my bag, but I was a second too late because that bitch whipped out a razor from her mouth and held it to my neck.

"Hold up. What are you doing?"

"Shut up, bitch! It's *my* turn to talk. I want one hundred grand to keep your little secret. You have two weeks to get it to me, or I'll be going to the police. No, better yet, I'll go to that nice man that was offering the reward. I think it's about time that someone teach your stuck-up behind a lesson."

The pressure that she was applying to my neck was getting to be unbearable. If only I could get to my gun, I would shoot this bitch right between the eyes. But I didn't move a muscle. I was terrified that if I did, I would startle her; plus, I wasn't sure what kind of drugs she was on at the time.

"Calm down. I'll do whatever you want me to do. Just move that thing away from my throat."

"Bitch, you can't trick me. This is not the movies. This is the real deal, and you *will* give me that money, or I *will* spill everything that I know."

"All right, I got it, okay? I'll call you with the money. You have my word."

"Your word? Save that for the niggas that are hunting you down, because, lady, I'm the least of your problems."

I wish that she would shut up and get the fucking blade off my neck. She must've read my mind because she removed the blade and immediately open the door and ran. I took a minute to catch my breath after all that pressure she placed on me. I watched as she jumped in her car and sped off. I wanted to chase her down and shoot her, but what good would that be? We were out in the open. People could say what they want, but Daddy ain't raised no fool. I know when to act and when to chill. I would get that bitch and kill her when the time was right!

Chapter Eleven

Alijah Jackson

Niggas always claimed they go hard, and oftentimes, I just sat back and observed the foolery. I lived and breathed this life. I knew I was living wrong, but that was all I knew. I really ain't got no education; the street was my college. I recall when Mom-dukes told me to get a job. I thought she was tripping 'cause from when I was a little yute, I was hustling; only back then, it was chump change. I was at a point now where I could contemplate walking away from the game. I planned on putting some of this illegal paper into buying a few Laundromats and maybe a few fast-food chains. Whatever I decide, it better be able to turn a profit.

Sierra decided that she didn't want to bounce with me; instead, she would come after she had the baby. Personally, I felt like it was bullshit. Out of the blue, she had this brand-new attitude.

I wasn't the type of nigga to trip over a bitch, but I do love shorty, so whatever she chose to do, well, I guess I'll just have to roll with it. I'll still make sure she and my seed were well taken care of. I needed her to know that I was going to be in my seed's life one way or another. If she ever tried to stop me from being a father, I won't have any choice but to body her.

I never met my pops and Mom-dukes never mentioned him. By the time I got older, I didn't give a fuck or care to know who the fucking sperm donor was. I don't want my seed to experience that, so I planned to make it my duty to be there, no matter what.

Things were wrapping up, and I was lying low. I barely drove, and if I had to go somewhere, Chuck or Dre did the driving. Richmond police were known for doing random spot checks, and I didn't want to fall victim to it.

I was ready to take this emergency trip up top. It was not on my agenda of things to do, but it was essential if I planned on moving forward. My two homies rolled with me, as always. Shayna kept playing hide-and-go-seek, so since I was tired of searching for that bitch, I decided to pay her parents a visit.

I knew that wicked bitch was somewhere cooking up some more drama. I was still in disbelief that she set me up and shot Sierra. I knew she was a lying, conniving bitch, but never thought she had the balls to go after me. I was ready to settle this once and for all.

The ride from VA to New York was spent rapping about business. We discussed our next move and how we were going to handle it. I respected the hell out of my partnas. They been down for me no matter what situation I happened to get myself in. There's never been a time that I could recall that I've ever had to question their loyalty. I knew without a doubt that they would ride until the breath left their bodies. I would do the same for them without question. After I lost Darryl, they really stepped it up and held me down.

I finally hit New York with one destination in mind, and that was Hempstead, Long Island. We finally arrived, and I drove a used car that I bought just for the sake of the trip into the gated community. I remembered the code that Shayna gave me years ago. I parked and got out of the car, walked up the driveway, and rang the bell. My niggas walked toward the back door. Mrs. Carter opened the door instantly, and as soon as she saw my face, I saw a look of displeasure plastered all over her chubby face.

"Honey, who's at the door?"

"It's Alijah, Shayna's husband," she yelled back before I had the chance to shut her up.

"It's your son-in-law. I need to talk to you." I moved past her and pushed the door shut.

"You can't just come in here. I'll call the police," Mr. Carter said upon entering the hall.

He took his cell phone off the clip from his waist and tried to dial a number. I was on point, though. I knocked it out of his hand. Then I pulled my gun from my waist and pointed it at his dome. His wife started to scream, so I had to move fast.

"Move over there, and you go ahead with him." I held the gun on both of them while I walked backward toward the back door and opened it up for my partners. I saw old dude's eyes pop open like he just realized shit was real.

Chuck gave me the rope, and I began to tie him to the chair. His wife continued to yell harder when Dre put his gun to her head. I tied the old man up and went over to her.

"Listen, Ms. Carter, you need to stop all this bloodclaat screaming right now." I looked her dead in the eyes, and if she was any good at reading people, she would sense that I meant business.

"What the hell you call yourself doing, coming up in here like this? Do you know *who* I am? I am well connected."

I used my gun and bust the old fart in the face. Blood squirted all over the place.

"OK, now you know who *I* am! Listen up, folks. I'm here for one thing, and one thing only. I want your daughter, but I see she's been ducking me. I know you good folks know where her ass has been hiding." I looked at both of them.

"Alijah, what in God's name is going on?"

"What's going on is I need you to call your daughter. Get the address of where she's staying at."

"Fuck you, you bastard! I warned Shayna about you years ago. I knew you weren't any good. I sat on that bench for over thirty years. I seen your kind on a daily basis."

I see this old nigga did not know when to shut his mouth.

"Oh, I hear you. I ain't no good. I'm a piece of shit, but your daughter didn't think that when I had my wood in her mouth. We could sit here and go back and forth, but I'm not here for all that." I handed him his phone. "Here you go. Call your daughter and get her address. You better not say a fucking word outside of what I tell you, and if you do, my partner is prepared to blow Delores's brains all over this kitchen."

"No, don't do this! I treated you like family. Please, Alijah," she pleaded. I saw the sincerity in her eyes, and it would have been a great script for Dr. Phil's show. However, I was not in the business of sincerity and emotions. I know that bitch was performing and was banking on the fact that she was a woman and that I would fall for the shit.

I raised my hand and slapped her across the face.

"Bitch, shut the fuck up! Tell him to do as I say, or I'ma blow your head off."

"Aubrey, please listen to him. I-I don't want to die," she wept.

"Delores, shut your friggin' mouth. I will not give in to this slimeball. She's my fucking daughter, and I will die before I utter a word."

I knew I had to go to the extreme to get this man's attention. I walked over to the door and got the bag that Chuck brought in. I took out my machete and walked over to the bitch.

"Let's try this one more time. Call your daughter."

"Please, Alijah, I don't have it. She changed her number. Please don't hurt us. We have money we can give you."

I placed my gun on my waist, took a step back, raised my machete, and chopped her head clean off her body. Blood splashed everywhere as the head fell to the ground, and her body, along with the chair, fell to the side.

The husband sat there frozen as he looked on as his wife's head bounced on the kitchen floor.

"No! No! No! No! You bastard! You killed her. You going to pay. I promise you will pay."

"Relax, old man. You're not on the judge's bench now. I'm in control. So, pussy hole, gi mi yuh daughter's number and her address."

He looked at me, hocked a wad, and spit. That shit landed in my face. I used my other hand and wiped it off. Dre rushed over, but I stopped him.

"Nah, bro! I got this. This bloodclaat ole man nuh know who him a deal with. Him 'bout fi find out, though."

I snatched the cell phone and scrolled through the contacts. There were no listings of that bitch's name. I cut it off and put it in my pocket. I took the rest of the tools out of the bag. It was his time to feel my wrath. I grabbed the saw and walked in front of him. I then placed it on his right knee and started sawing through it, pretending like it was fresh oxtail's bones.

I tuned out the screaming by the old fool. His bones were old, so it took a little longer to saw the leg off.

"Noooooooooooo! Nooooo! Stop, oh, Jehovah God, please stop."

"Too late, pussy hole, now give me the fucking info and *maybe* I'll spare your other leg," I lied.

"Go to hell. I'm ready to die. Just kill me, you punk. Go ahead, kill me."

While he was busy talking that bullshit, I started on the left knee. The yelling got louder. I sped up the process and cut off the other leg. It was a bloody situation. His face wore the expression of extreme pain. The fool still wouldn't give up any info; instead, he kept mumbling and praying to God. I came to the realization that he'd die for his daughter, so it was waste of my time. I took my Glock out and fired two shots in his face, dividing his brain meat into tiny particles.

After that, I put on a pair of gloves and searched the house thoroughly. There was no information anywhere about Shayna or her whereabouts. We cleaned up and made sure there was no evidence of us ever being there. It was already dark outside, so we slipped through the back door and drove off into the night.

Each killing that I did was becoming easier than the last. The thrill I got from seeing my victims' faces when they knew they were about to meet their Maker was priceless.

I knew I didn't get what I came for, but by the time people find the bodies, Shayna will be out of hiding, and believe me, I will get that ass. Dre stayed behind at a nearby hotel, and Chuck and I drove back to the South. She will walk right into the trap that I set for her.

Shayna Jackson

The last couple of days have been stressful. I was shocked that the crackhead really tried me like that. She wanted a hundred grand. I thought about not giving that bitch a penny, but I couldn't really gamble with it. I was not scared of the feds knowing, because they already were on to me. My concern was her telling the dude she claimed was asking questions. I'm pretty sure he was one of Alijah's people. I was concerned that if I paid her, she would smoke it up, and then come back for more.

So many decisions to make, so little time. I had to figure out how to shut this bitch up for good. After a lot of soul searching and brain torturing, I decided not to give that bitch a dime. I was going to play along like I was ready to pay her, and when she shows up for her money, I'd pay her in full—with a bullet in her head.

I wished the grand jury would hurry up and come back with the indictment. That way, they can pick up Alijah, because unless he was picked up, my life was in danger. After his trial, I planned to leave the state. I didn't like this old country-ass, racist state anyway. Money was my only motivation for coming here, and nothing played out the way that I envisioned it. Here I was in a whole bunch of mess, all because of that no-good-ass nigga. Things would've been different if he had just been a perfect husband; but, no, he couldn't control his cock, and now he shall pay with his freedom.

I recalled when he used to accuse me of trying to control his life. Little did he know that when he does get to prison, his life will be literally controlled by the Federal Bureau of Prison guards. Oh well, we'll see how the big bad Alijah Jackson adjusts to life in the real big house.

I've been calling my parents for the last few days, and the calls have been going directly to voice mail. That was so unlike Daddy. We spoke on Saturday, and I was supposed to call him on Wednesday, and it was Saturday again. A whole week had gone by. He knew my current situation and would not have gone out of town without telling me first. I had a bad feeling in the pit of my stomach. It was strange that both my parents' phones were turned off at the same time. I was willing to give it until tomorrow, or I will be calling the Hempstead police so they could do a welfare check on them.

I tried to sleep. I twisted and turned all night. I felt an anxiety attack creeping up on me. I haven't had one of those since my college days. I remembered the feeling; my palms got sweaty, and my chest started to tighten up. I can't breathe. "Oh, God, help me. I-I can't take this," I whispered. I remembered what the nurse at my college told me to do. I crawled in the corner of the room, counted to ten slowly, and then I counted backward. I breathed slowly. I tried to control it. I started to breathe slower, and I finally had it under control. I stayed there until I dozed off.

I was awakened by the sun beaming in through the curtain. I knew it was daytime, and I needed to get up. I had to find my daddy; all we had was each other. I showered, got dressed, and grabbed my purse and car keys. I was heading home to find my daddy!

The streets were scarce with cars, so I used that to my advantage. At times, I touched 100 miles per hour. It took me five-and-a-half hours to get to the Lincoln Tunnel and into my home state. My entire journey, I begged God to protect my parents. I knew I wasn't close to God, but I needed him, and from the little that I knew about him, he was very understanding.

I entered the city, and five minutes later, I pulled into my parents' driveway. I saw the nosy neighbor peeping out the front window. I paid him no mind, but something caught my attention. Both of my parents' cars were in the driveway, and the newspapers were piled up on the doorstep. That was also strange. Every morning, the first thing that Daddy did was get dressed and got the newspaper from outside. He would then sit at the table reading the morning news and drink a cup of coffee. This was his daily routine from as far back as I could remember. I rang the doorbell multiple times. There was no answer, so I started to bang on the door.

"Daddy, it's me. Open the door." I banged harder.

"Mama, it's me, Shayna. If you're in there, open the door." The entire plea was in vain.

I walked over to the neighbor's house, and he opened the door before I could even ring the bell.

"Hello, pretty lady," he said with that crooked smile.

"Hello. I was wondering, have you seen or spoken to my parents lately?"

"I haven't seen them come or go for 'bout a week. I just figured they were gone up to Peekskill. You know they usually go up there 'round this time of the year."

"Doesn't that strike you as strange, since Daddy always asks you to watch the house while he's out of town?" I asked.

"Right! Right! I saw them come home from dinner, but I must've missed them when they left."

"Did you call his phone?"

"Yes, I have been calling him for a couple of days, but the calls are going straight to voice mail."

"Well, I'm going to go over and see if I can get in."

"Oh, hold on! I have a spare key that Aubrey gave me."

He went inside to get the key. I didn't like the old pervert, but he was being helpful at the moment.

"Here you go. I'll walk with you over there just in case you need me, pretty lady," he said while he batted his grey eyelashes at me.

I wanted to smack that old, wicked, perverted smile off his face; instead, I ignored him and walked out of his yard and into my parents' yard.

He followed closely behind. I used the key and opened the door. Instantly, I was greeted with a foul odor. I pushed the door opened and step foot inside. The place smelled like an animal had died in there. I took a quick glance around—that's when I saw the most horrible sight in my life. There were two bodies on the ground, with body parts beside them.

I ran out screaming, snatched my cell out of my purse, and called the police.

"9-1-1, what's your emergency?"

"I found two bodies in my parents' home. Please hurry, send the police," I screamed in the phone.

"Ma'am, what's your parents' address?"

"It's 2015 Vahorn Street. Please hurry," I pleaded.

I got down on my knees on the cold concrete. My feet wouldn't hold my weight. I was trembling so hard, I didn't hear another word that the operator was saying. I just kept screaming and screaming.

Within three minutes I heard police sirens, fire trucks, and the ambulance coming down the street. I tried to get up, but I couldn't. The old man wrapped his nasty old hands around my waist and gave me support so I could stand up.

"Ma'am, is this your residence?"

"No, my parents live here."

"OK, ma'am, can you give me your name and the names and ages of your parents?"

I pulled myself together long enough to give him the information. There wasn't too much I could give to them. All I knew was that I've been calling them for a week and got no reply. There were police everywhere; crime scene investigators also pulled up. I was no expert, but I knew they were dead!

I was too scared to go inside, even when they asked me to identify the bodies. The neighbor was nice enough to do that part. I already knew in my heart it was them. The detective told me that they've been dead for quite a while, but he would wait on the coroner to confirm the exact time of death.

"Ma'am, do you know of anyone that would harm your parents?"

"No, not off the top of my head. Daddy is a retired judge, and Mama stayed at home."

"Do you live here?"

"No, I live in Virginia. I've been calling them and got no answer, so I came up here to check on them."

"I'll need to get some more info from you; your whereabouts, etc. . . . . other family members and close friends who have access to the home."

"OK, whatever," I said with an attitude.

I would never harm my daddy, but then again, the detective would never understand the relationship between me and my daddy. I didn't care about his investigation. Someone killed them, and I want to know who and why.

"This is a murder investigation. I'll wait on the medical examiner to give me the exact cause of death and time; then I'll proceed. My guys are searching for evidence right now."

"What do you mean? Some asshole came up in here and killed my parents, and you want to drag your feet? Fuck that. I need to talk to your boss."

"Ma'am, I'm following procedure, and you yourself couldn't even identify the bodies. I know you're upset, but let us handle this. Trust me, we will find the killer or killers responsible for this."

All that damn talking didn't mean a thing to me. I wanted my daddy back. Don't get me wrong, I loved Mama and all, but my daddy was my everything. He was the only one that never judged me. He accepted my flaws and all. He never raised his voice at me and was always there to tell me everything was going to be all right. Just the other day when we talked, I told him about Alijah and the feds' investigation.

He comforted me and was getting ready to buy me a place out in Phoenix, Arizona.

I was overcome with grief, and my thoughts were all over the place. I never imagined burying my parents, but I had no choice. I spent the next two hours talking with the detective and watching them bag up evidence from the crime scene. The coroner removed the bodies, and they left.

I still couldn't go in, so I locked the door and drove to the closest Marriott. I needed to be alone in a dark room where I could let all my emotions flow without interruption. I walked through the door and threw my key and purse on the bed. I crawled in the bed; then this song popped in my head: *"Amazing grace! How sweet the sound, that saved a wretch like me! I once was lost, but now am found; was blind, but now I see."* This was Daddy's favorite song that he used to sing to me when I was a little girl. I sang the entire song as the tears poured out. My heart was burning with grief.

Life wasn't supposed to be this hard. I needed all the pain to go away. I wished that I was there to protect my daddy. Instead, I was cooped up in a hotel room while my daddy was being tortured. What animal would cut them up like that? I couldn't imagine!

***

I received a call from the detective. He called to inform me that the coroner confirmed it was my parents. That wasn't a surprise. I already knew that. He also notified me the autopsy will be done in a few days; then the bodies will be released to me. I notified a few family members. Most of them didn't care; they only cared about what my parents could do for them. For everyone else, Channel Seven News brought the story, so I'm pretty sure they saw it.

I decided not to have a funeral; instead, I would cremate them. I also had a lot of business arrangements to take care of. It hit me that I was the sole beneficiary of all Daddy's money. I had to make sure I go through all the finances and contact all his business partners.

The next few days were very hard for me. I called a cleaning company so they could clean out the house. I couldn't return until all the blood was gone. I planned on selling the house when everything calmed down. I couldn't live in there after what happened.

The coroner stated that Mama's head was chopped off with a sharp knife or machete, and she was also beaten severely. Daddy was tortured, and his legs were cut off. And if that wasn't bad enough, he was shot twice in the face. The detective called the killing personal and gruesome.

A quick thought popped in my mind when he mentioned machete. There was only one person that I knew that owned a few, and that was Alijah. I was with him on a few different occasions when he bought them. With that bit of knowledge, I felt my body shiver. I wondered if he was responsible for this. Were their killings revenge for me giving him up to the authorities, and was this a way to get my attention? Daddy did tell me that Alijah called a month back inquiring about my whereabouts. If my suspicion was true, I knew I wasn't safe. He might be lurking around just waiting on the right opportunity to present itself.

I knew I was no match for him and his goons, so I need to be extra careful. I dialed Sanders's number to inform him about the death of my parents and about my suspicion. He wasn't of much help. He told me to come to VA. Really? Did that son of a bitch hear *anything* that I said to him? I think not! Fuck him, fuck the feds, fuck the crackhead bitch, and most of all, fuck Alijah and his bitch.

I was going to get myself out of all this chaos, but first things first. I had my parents' bodies cremated and put into matching purple urns. Purple was Daddy's favorite color. I can take them with me wherever I plan on moving to.

That way, they won't be alone, and I'll have my daddy close by, just like old times.

Everything was wrapped up in a few days. Then I headed back to VA. I had a few loose ends to tie up there; then I planned on making my grand appearance when I testified against my husband. I will then buy me a one-way ticket out of the country. I was thinking the Cayman Islands. I heard they were beautiful. After all, I will be rich and will be able to live my life the way it should be lived.

Sierra Rogers

Jeanette finally called me and said she was ready to take me up on my offer. I went to pick her up. To be honest, by the time she called, I was starting to have doubts. I didn't know how it was going to work out between us, but I was determined to try.

I arrived at Whitcomb, and she was waiting outside with her black garbage bags. Ironically, it was the same kind of bag that she had when she left me many years ago. I felt my emotions trying to creep down that dark memory lane, but I quickly shook off the feeling. I popped the trunk, and she threw her bags in and got in the car.

"Hey, girl, thanks for picking me up. I can't tell you how much I appreciate this, and I promise I won't let you down."

"I'm too old for people to let me down. But I'm warning you, don't bring no drugs in my home, and the first time I feel any type of feeling that you're using again, I am throwing yo' ass out. You hear me?"

"Sierra, God is my witness, I am clean."

"That's what all crackheads say," I mumbled under my breath before I pulled off.

I showed her around the house and led her to the fully furnished room she'd be living in. I watched as her eyes lit up as she entered the room. She rubbed her hand across the forty-two-inch plasma TV that was on the stand beside her bed. I left as she began to unpack her clothes.

That night, she asked if she could cook dinner. I didn't see any reason why not, so I agreed. She made baked chicken with baked potatoes, gravy, and green beans. This was my first time eating something she cooked, or more like the first time that I remember. I had to give credit where it was due, she did the damn thing in the kitchen, and the food was so good. My pregnant ass ate and went back for seconds. I could really get used to this, but I had to be careful. I didn't want to put on a lot of weight. I need my hourglass shape back as soon as possible after I dropped the baby.

The day came when we got to find out the sex of our baby. I was praying for a girl, and Alijah was praying for a boy. We haven't spoken much since our heated argument. This day was different. We walked into the doctor's office like the proud parents that we were. Everything seemed fine with the baby, who was busy moving around. It was confirmed that we were having a boy. I was a little disappointed, but I was okay with it as long as I have a healthy baby. Alijah was gloating with happiness as he finally got his wish.

After the doctor's appointment, he asked me to join him for lunch. I said yes because it was a happy day, and I didn't want to rain on his parade by turning him down. Truth was, I really missed our closeness. Ever since I found out I was pregnant, I couldn't stand to be around him or inhale his scent. There was something about his scent that made me nauseated. I really do miss the bond that we once shared. Maybe one day we could rekindle our flame that was so hot and bright once upon a time.

I was too caught up in my thoughts to realize that he took me to The Caribbean Pot, the same restaurant that we went to on our first date. We had not been back since then. The setting was still the same; it was cozy and comfortable. We were seated close to the back, which I believe he requested. I wasn't sure why, so I left it alone.

We ordered our meal, and he ordered wine for himself and water for me. The waitress was on point, and we started to eat in complete silence.

"Why you looking at me like that?"

"Just looking at your beauty."

"Really? I thought you been saw that."

"Yea, I did, but some reason, you are glowing right now."

"Mmm-hmm. I don't feel like it. I feel so bloated."

"Ain't nothing wrong wit' you, B. You are even more beautiful when you're pregnant."

"Boy, whatever. You haven't paid me no mind, and then all of a sudden, now you can't take your eyes off me."

He reached across the table and grabbed my hand and held it in his. "Listen, B! I kno' lately I haven't been the best, but that don't mean that I don't love you. You're the only woman outside of Mom-dukes that I love. I kno' sometimes it's hard to deal with me, but, shorty, I fucking love you."

"You love me, but you're fucking around on me. That ain't love. I deserve better than you are dishing out."

"I mean, I'ma keep it one hunnit with you. I'm a dude, so, yes, I do love to fuck different pussy, but I 'ont give a fuck 'bout none a dem hoes. Yuh a mi wife."

"Wow! You believe that I am supposed to be satisfied with that? I'm not and can't pretend. I am not going to act like shit sweet."

"I'm not asking you to. Let's admit it; we both fucked up, so let's put it behind us and move forward."

"Boy, whatever. I ain't tryna hear that shit," I said and tried to snatch my hand away from his tight grip.

"Sierra, leave with me. I need you and my seed. We can make a life together."

"Alijah, you're wanted. I can't put me and my child through that. I just can't."

"Yo, B. You have me feeling some type of way, but I promise you that if you leave with me, I will give up the streets. I will give everything up. I swear."

"Ha-ha! You are too funny. You're not leaving the streets. Save that lie for one of your bitches."

"Man, I am dead-ass serious. I put that on my li'l man. I need y'all in my life. Let's raise our baby together."

"You want me to just up and leave my house and my shop?"

"Fuck that shit. Leave the house with your mama, and I'll buy you a bigger and better house."

I wanted to go with him, regardless of how mad he made me. He was the only man that ever treated me like somebody. I did not want to lose him or risk my son not having his father in his life. I started to cry. Everything was so messed up. I just want it fixed. I wanted to go back to when I first met him; the laughter and the happiness. I wonder if I let him go, how I would know if we could've made it to the place that we were before. I need to know! I *have* to know!

"OK, Alijah, I will go, but I want to have my baby here; then I need a few extra weeks to wrap up some things."

"A'ight. Bet. I'll wait until you have the baby; then you can come. Ma, I really appreciate you giving me another chance. I won't fuck up."

"You better not, because this is your last fucking chance. I will leave your ass the next time you cheat on me. I am dead-ass serious." I gritted my face at him.

We talked for a little while longer, then he paid, and we left. I was happy that we had a chance to really talk. It was long needed; there was too much animosity in the previous days that was weighing heavily on both of us. I had doubts that he was going to leave the streets alone, but only time will tell if he does. I hope he meant it, because if he doesn't, he will pay for lying.

We arrived home and saw that all the lights were off. I guess Jeanette went to bed early. I took a shower, and he took one after me. We both got in bed and held each other; no words, no sex. We bonded like we haven't seen each other in years. I sure missed that feeling of just lying up with him.

I had the baby's crib set up in my room. There was no way I was going to let him out of my sight. I ordered so many designer clothes for him, it was a shame UPS was making deliveries every day to the same address. Jeanette was helpful around the house. She made sure all the baby's clothing was washed and folded. I figured she was feeling somewhat guilty that she wasn't present in my life, so she was trying to do better this time around. I really thought that I would feel weird having her around, but I wasn't. I did notice that whenever I was at home, she'd lock herself in her room. I guess trying to stay out of the way.

*****

Today, I was lying in my bed. It seems like the closer that I got to my due date the more tired I became. I was on the countdown to push out my little man. My phone started ringing over and over. I lay there trying to ignore it, but whoever it was wasn't trying to let up. I eventually snatched it off the bed and answered it.

"Hello," I said in a harsh tone.

"Sierra, it's me."

"Me who?" I looked at the caller ID to see if I recognized the number, but I did not.

"Girl, it's Neisha. Your best friend, silly."

"What the fuck you want? You ain't no motherfucking friend of mine," I spat.

"Sierra, calm down. I need to meet you. I have something to tell you."

My antennas went up immediately. I knew she was the only one that I gave my address to, and I put my life on it she gave it to Shayna. I wasn't sure how their paths crossed, but I know it did. I needed to know how, where, and why. It was time to pay back these to bitches in full.

"Hmm . . . What is it you want to tell me?" I said a more somber tone.

"Charley told me that your memory of the shooting is gone, and I have an idea of who it might be."

"Really? Shut your mouth and keep on talking."
I said this phrase when we used to hang.

"I was thinking that maybe we could meet, sit
down, and talk like old times."

"Okay, what do you have in mind?"

"I have my own little place over here on Broad
Rock Road. Nothing fancy. I figure I could throw
some turkey wings in the oven until you get here.
You know you love how I cook them."

"Bet! Sounds great to me. Give me a minute
to get dressed and I'll be on the way." I took the
address and hung up.

I remained seated on the bed for a second
so I could let all this marinate. This ho is really
brave—or she's just plain stupid. Either way,
I get to see the enemy. I did not consider her
anything less. I got up and got dressed in all-
black Aeropostale sweatpants and jacket. I then
took my gun out from under the pillow and
checked to make sure it was loaded. I went into
my drawer and took out an extra clip and put it
in my Gucci bag.

I thought about calling Alijah to let him know
where I was heading, but I dismissed that idea. I
needed to handle this by myself. I snuck downstairs. I didn't want Jeanette to hear me leaving.
I headed to the garage and grabbed a few things
that might come in handy. You never know what
might pop off with that sheisty bitch.

Then I got in my car and drove off. I got to the South, and in no time, I spotted the address that she gave me and pulled in the yard. I was feeling butterflies in my stomach, and my guard was up. I held my bag close to me, just in case.

She opened the door before I had a chance to knock. The first thought that came to my mind is this bitch is pressed.

"Come in, *chica*. Now look at you. Stomach all big," she said with a china grin.

I stepped inside . . . and into a house of filth. Her ass lied about having her own place. The house was nothing but a smitty, a house that crackheads and dopefiends take over and turn it in to their own. The place smelled like shit and chicken mixed together with stinking pussy, a very terrible combination.

"Girl, sit down. You carrying a load," she said, then pointed to an old sofa that had brown stains all over the worn-out cloth material.

"No, I'm fine. I've been lying down all day, so a little standing ain't goin' hurt nothing."

"OK, the food is almost done; then we can eat."

"I hear you. So what did you want to talk about?" I asked with a slight attitude. I was tired of all the bullshit small talk about irrelevant bullshit.

"Girl, you know, I met Alijah's wife, Shayna." She looked at me for a reaction.

"So?" I shrugged my shoulders.

"Well, friend, let me tell you. I think she's the one that shot you."

"What would make you think such a thing?"

"She's a grimy bitch; plus, from the way she talks, I know she's jealous of you."

This bottom feeding bitch went on to tell me how they met, all their later interactions, but not one time did she mention how she betrayed me or the fact that she was the one that gave her my address. I looked at her as I thought of my next move. I stood there thinking how blind I had been not to see her for the jealous, conniving bitch that she was.

"Neisha, I have a question for you."

"What, girl?"

"When did you start hating on me, and how much was our friendship worth?"

"Whatchu mean? What I need to hate on you fo'?"

"You tell me. We were like sisters, wore the same clothes, even shared the same drawers sometimes. Fucked the same niggas. So I'm curious, when did you start hating on me?"

By this time, tears welled into my eyes. I was crying because I was hurt.

"You right, we're tight. That's when yo' ass was one of us, but the second you met that Jamaican nigga, you got all high and mighty, like yo' shit don't stink. You turned your back on me," she yelled.

"Turn my back? Bitch, I've always helped you. I bought you clothes, put money in your pocket. I have a pussy, you have a pussy. I decide to use mine to my advantage, and you decide to fuck for free. Don't fucking blame me because you were too fucking stupid to profit off yours," I yelled back.

"Sierra, please miss me with that bullshit. You got lucky, but trust me, that nigga will soon find out that he can't turn a ho into a housewife, and when he does, your ass will be just another old ho that got used up by the dope boy," she said before walking into the kitchen.

I took that moment to get my .38 revolver out of my bag. I held it behind my bag until she came back in the front room.

"Neisha, you see, I've always been the one not to trust bitches. So, while I *am* disappointed, I am not shocked that you would hate on me. I remember when I first told you about Alijah, I heard the jealousy in your tone. That was the moment I knew I couldn't trust you."

I raised my gun and stepped closer to her.

"You see, I know you gave that bitch my address, and you have the nerve to act like you're not responsible for me getting shot. You're just as guilty as the bitch that pulled the trigger."

"You can't be serious pulling a gun on me. I see you been hanging around that boy too much."

"Bitch, shut the fuck up. This ain't no fucking joke—"

I did not get a chance to finish my sentence. That crazy bitch leaped toward me. She had a big advantage over me because I had a big-ass stomach in front of me. I couldn't really fight the way that I wanted to. She knocked me to the ground and jumped on top of my stomach. It was then my maternal instinct kicked in. I grabbed that heifer's neck and brought my left hand up, and without hesitation, I squeezed the trigger. I hit her in the neck.

I watched as her eyes widened, and she looked at me. I used all my strength and pushed her off me. She was choking on her own blood as she fought for her life. I stood up and aimed my gun and fired a single shot into her heart that killed her instantly.

I stood there in a trance for a minute. This was my first killing, and I was shaking terribly. I quickly snapped out of it. I needed to think fast before anyone showed up. I've always known that I was going to kill her; just never planned it out. I needed to figure out what I was going to do with the body because I was standing in the middle of the floor with a dead bitch and the murder weapon in my hand.

I felt like throwing up, and before the thought left my mind, I *was* throwing up on the dead body. Then I started having cold sweats all over my body. Next, I felt a gush of water leaking down my legs. My first guess was I was so nervous I peed on myself. I then recalled what the doctor said would happen when my water broke. I stuck my finger between my legs and felt a sticky, watery substance.

I knew I needed to act fast. I dialed Alijah's phone number. He picked up on the first ring.

"Hey, boo."

"What's good? Just swung by the house but you were gone."

"Yea, listen, I need you and your peoples to swing by and clean up for me."

"Bet! Give me the address; we on the way," he said without hesitation. That was a code we had in place in case I ever got myself in any sticky situation.

"Boo, hurry, my water just broke. I need to get to the hospital."

"You mean our baby is on the way? You need to bounce, go to the hospital. I'ma handle that situation; then I'll be there. Johnson Willis, right?"

"Yes, it's not far from here." I gave him the address and hung up.

I snuck out the half-broken back door and got into my car. As soon as I did, I began to feel weak and wasn't sure I was going to make it. I looked down at my clothes to check for any visible sign of blood. I realized my jacket was soaked with blood, so I took it off. I put the gun and the jacket into a plastic bag. I popped my trunk and placed them in there. I need Alijah to hurry up because the gun was registered in my name, and I threw up all over the bitch, so that can be traced back to me. I was nervous and scared. Now I see why I wasn't a born killer.

By then, I was in a lot of pain, so I pulled out of the yard. I saw Alijah in my rearview mirror pulling in, so I backed up and popped my trunk.

"Boo, get that out of my trunk," I hollered.

He jumped out of the car, went to the trunk, and got the bag. I was going to report the gun stolen in the morning. I sped off to the hospital. I called Mo', but she did not pick up, so I called Jeanette. I didn't want her to think I needed her, but considering all that I've been through today,

I just need someone to be in the delivery room with me.

I was excited and nervous, all in one. The doctors said they had to induce my labor because my water broke, but the baby wasn't ready. Hours later, Alijah showed up holding my hand. Jeanette was also there for support.

It wasn't until nine the next morning that I started to have contractions, and, boy, those pains were nothing compared to other pains that I have felt before. I chose to not get an epidural because of the horror stories from other chicks about how you'll get back pain in the future. Nah, I decided to go the natural way.

At exactly 12:45 p.m., my little man made his grand entrance into this world. The nurse placed him in my arms. As I looked him in the eyes, I started to cry tears of joy. He was the most beautiful human being that I ever laid eyes on. I saw the happiness on his father's face as he walked over to us. He stood there staring at us like he was just in awe. Jeanette was standing there, smiling from ear to ear.

It was definitely a day that changed all our lives. This was the day that Azir Anthony Jackson entered this cruel world. He was seven pounds

and five ounces. I whispered a silent prayer to
God thanking him and asking him to send his
angels to protect my little man.

The nurse came and took him to the nursery. I
was reluctant to let him out of my sight; however,
after a little reassurance, I let him go. His daddy
was so happy that he kept thanking me. He was
glowing that he finally got his wish. He had a
"mini-me."

I needed to talk to Alijah alone, so I asked
Jeanette to leave the room. I really didn't know
her and damn sure wasn't going to trust her.

"Boo, did you handle everything?" I asked.

"I told you I gotcha. You ain't got nothing to
worry 'bout. Relax, girl."

"I'm just asking, that's all."

"I gotcha. I live this life. Trust me, everything
is gone. Cleaned out completely."

"Okay, now I can finally breathe."

"Yea, next time, let me handle some shit like
that. I need you home with my little man, not
out being a thug," he said and poked me in the
arm.

"I know, boo. This shit is just crazy. I can't
believe this happened."

"Shh. Tell me about it later. Right now, you
need to relax. You just did the most amazing
thing in the world, and that's giving birth. All
that other shit is irrelevant."

"You're right about that. I'm starved. I feel like I could eat a cow right now."

"What you tryna eat?"

"Not sure. Umm, maybe some KFC."

"Bet. I have something to handle real quick; then I'll get your food." He kissed me on the forehead.

"OK, I'll be here."

He left, and Jeanette entered the room. I was not in the mood to talk. I was mentally and physically drained. I just killed a bitch and gave birth, all in a twenty-four span.

"Sierra, the nurses wanted to come in and clean you up, but I told them I'd do it, if you don't mind."

"That's fine; you can do it."

She helped me wash up, and I changed into my nightgown. She then left and told me she'd be back in the morning. I got back into bed, then called for the nurse to inquire about my son. She told me she'd bring him in shortly. I was getting irritated. I wanted to know why in God's name they had my baby that long. Shit, it's *my* child.

I finally got to see my baby. I took him out of the hospital bassinet and held him in my arms. It was time to feed him, and I had decided not to breast-feed. So, I used one of the Enfamil samples the hospital provided. I watched him closely as he took his tiny little sucks of the nipple from the bottle. It was just amazing that I brought this precious life into existence.

He ate and went straight to sleep. I was tired too, even though I tried to stay up so I could eat. I know Alijah said he had something to handle real quick, but it's been awhile since he left. I dialed his number, and it went straight to voice mail. I hung up the phone and lay my head on the pillow.

Chapter Twelve

Alijah Jackson

The birth of my son was astounding. I knew Sierra wanted a girl, but I didn't. I wanted a li'l man that I could teach about different things in life. Being around when he popped out of her pussy was odd to me. I had to give it to shorty; she's one strong woman.

My love for her has just skyrocketed. She gave me a son, and there's no way I could thank her enough. Standing there looking at both of them just validated my decision to leave the streets alone. I've never thought in a million years that I would walk away from this life, but I had too much to lose if I didn't. I just can't risk losing my family.

I've been schooling Chuck and Dre on e'erything 'bout the business. I was confident that they could handle it, even though I was walking away from the daily interactions. I would still be making certain calls, just not that much. I decided to throw some of the illegal money into real estate. The market was booming, so that's a tight investment, along with some Laundromats in New York which was a business that will never get slow because people up top are always doing laundry.

I received a text from Dre and left the hospital immediately. I called him so I could know what's going on. I thought Shayna would've been dead already, but he informed me that the place was swarming with police, and it wouldn't be a wise decision to move on her at that moment. I trusted my man's instinct. I also learned that he followed her back to VA, and she was staying at the Marriott on Broad Street.

That was great news because I needed to get at her. Her ass done did enough damage, and it was time for her to pay her dues.

This was a hotel that stayed busy, so I knew we were going to take a big chance going up in there. Fuck it, we just had to be extra careful. I couldn't rest until this bitch was six feet under!

***

Shayna Jackson

My entire life, I've never been without my daddy. He was the one that taught me how to ride my first bike; how to throw a ball and how to shoot. Losing him really hurt my heart. I know no other man can replace my daddy, even if they tried.

The day that I arrived at my parents' house, I had a strange feeling like someone was watching me from a distance. I shook the feeling because I was caught up in my grief. My fears were confirmed on my way back to Virginia. I saw a car in my rearview mirror when I went through the tunnel. It probably wouldn't have caught my attention if the license plate wasn't from VA. At one point, I sped up some. The car sped up too. I managed to get two cars ahead. The entire ride through Delaware, the car sat on my tail.

I called Sanders's phone to let him know that I was being followed. Within minutes, the feds were calling me. They instructed me to stay calm and continue on my journey. I wasn't sure, but I had a strong feeling that it was Alijah or one of his boys. I tried to get a glimpse inside of the car, but the windows were tinted.

I wasn't going to put my life in the hands of the feds, even though it was in their best interest to protect their star witness. I kept my cool all the way back to the hotel. As I pulled into the parking lot, I saw the black two-door sedan parking on the side. I checked for my gun in my purse, just in case I needed to use it. Luckily, I made it to my room without any incident.

The feds were so fucking slick. Before I got there, they already had a room occupied adjacent to mine. I almost jumped out of my skin when I got the phone call from them, telling me to open the interior door beside the bathroom door. I stood there in surprise when I saw a number of federal agents entering my room.

I was later briefed that there was a hit on my life, and Alijah and his crew might be coming after me in the hotel. They also told me that they were sure that he was responsible for my parents' death. I felt rage and wanted to kill the bastard my damn self. I also felt guilty for bringing that animal into their lives. A tear dropped down my face as I grieved my daddy.

I stayed in the room next door with two agents while the others remained in my room waiting for Alijah and his boys to show up. I hope they were right this time around, because I was ready for this phase of my life to end, and I pray sooner than later!

Chapter Thirteen

Alijah Jackson

We met up in the Marriott's parking lot. Chuck and Dre were present, along with Damion. This was his first time rolling with us on something this major. He was still new to my team, and I hadn't yet built that type of trust with him. He insisted on going on this run so he could prove his loyalty and commitment to the crew. I said fuck it and gave him a chance to see if he was really built for this life.

We discussed how we were going to enter the building without bringing any extra attention on us. We came up with the perfect plan on how to go about it. All three of them got out first and walked into the hotel. I waited five minutes, then got out with my briefcase in hand. I was disguised as an Arab businessman. I fit right in with the heavy traffic of businessmen walking in the lobby.

The plan was for Chuck to get entry into her hotel room as the maintenance man. Everything was working out as planned. I took the elevator to the second floor, heading to room 212B. My guns, silencer, and gloves were all in my briefcase. I was eager to get to the room. I wanted to see the look on her face when she realized she was being ambushed.

I knew that they were already in the room because one of them would've called if there was any type of surprise. I received no call, so that was definitely a go for me. I was the only person on the elevator, which was a plus; couldn't risk any witnesses. The elevator stopped, and I stepped into the hallway. Room 212B was toward my left, so I turned and walked down the hallway.

My feet were moving, but I was dragging. As I approached closer to the door, I had a sudden feeling that I was being watched. I had a real bad feeling about entering that room. I heard Saleem's voice in my head, *"Follow your gut instinct."* My first instinct was telling me to turn around and bounce the fuck up outta there. But I couldn't. My niggas were up in there because of me. I needed to know what's going on, so I walked up to the door and knocked on it.

The door popped open, and about a dozen U.S. Marshals rushed me from all angles with their guns drawn. Damn it! It was a setup.

"Get down! Get down! U.S. Marshals! Get down on the ground. Do not move!"

One of them pushed me down to the ground.

"Alijah Jackson, you're under arrest."

"For what?"

"Murder, attempted murder, gun possession, conspiracy, drug trafficking across state lines, possession of a firearm while in the course of committing a crime, and the list goes on."

I looked at this bitch as she read the charges to me. The other fed dude cuffed me and searched my waist. They then picked me up off the ground. I finally got to see all the motherfucking pigs that rushed me. They were lucky that the cuffs were on me because I wanted to punch those motherfuckers in the face.

I saw when they led Chuck and Dre out in the cuffs, and then I noticed that Damion wasn't cuffed. What the fuck? My mind was racing.

"Yo, son, what's going on?"

That pussy hole stepped closer to my face. "I am not your son. I am Federal Agent Somers," he said. "I'm an undercover agent, and I've been investigating you and your criminal empire."

"Ha-ha!" All I could do was laugh. This nigga is the fucking feds. I ate with this nigga, broke bread with this nigga, and he was the fucking law.

For the first time in my entire life, I was at a loss for words. I just stood there thinking of all the different ways that I could kill that bomboclaat clown. I was shocked that my niggas and I just delivered ourselves to them. I couldn't even get away; there was three of us and around thirty of them bitches.

The walk from the hotel hallway through the back entrance to the paddy wagon was the longest walk of my life. All my thoughts were diverted to Sierra and my son. She was expecting me to return with her food. I know she'd be worrying by now.

I needed to call her so she could be on point. I wasn't sure she wasn't wrapped up in all this bullshit. I done brought this nigga in my life, not knowing he was an informer. Only Jah know what he done reported on us.

They put us in the van; this gave me some time to rap with my niggas and to get a better understanding of what the hell happened when they got to the room. I was curious to know why I didn't get any phone call warning of a possible setup.

"Brethren, what happen?"

"Son, it was a setup from the gate. Shayna ass went in that room, but I guess they were on to us because they switched rooms with her, because she never left out," Chuck said.

"Boss, I felt it as soon as I entered the room, they were waiting on us, but what fucked me up the most is when dude pulled his gun on us. I froze up, because I didn't see it coming."

"Well, my niggas, shit don't look good. I have to get in touch with Saleem and Sierra; we have to get these lawyers in. I doubt we goin' get a bond, but it's worth trying."

"Boss, they mentioned Saleem's name when we were in the room. I believe they're about to pick him up."

I raised my foot and kicked the window of the van. I should've killed Shayna years ago. I should've done a million things, but don't none of that shit matter at the moment. I knew I had little or no chance against the federally, but I was going to fight with e'erything in me. I owe it to my mama, Sierra, and my little man.

I looked over at my partners, and I peeped the sadness all over their faces. I knew they've been in this life since they were young and don't nothing really faze them. So to see them looking like that really cut me deep. This was some sucka shit. It was like we didn't even let these niggas work for their checks. We just walked right in and delivered ourselves. That one move might seal our fate!

Sierra Rogers

It was midnight, and there's still no sign of Alijah. I called his phone over thirty times, and all I was getting was the voice mail. I left him over five messages and still no callback. That was not like him, especially when he left, he knew I was hungry and was waiting to eat.

I tried not to get all worked up, but the shit seemed unreal. I called Jeanette to see if he dropped by the house, but she hadn't seen him since he left the hospital. I didn't have anyone else's number to call, so I lay there hoping he would walk into the room any minute.

I needed to find him, but here I was in bed, laid up. My pussy was hurting from the twelve stitches I had from pushing too hard. I wasn't scheduled to be discharged until the next day. I sat up in the bed pondering my next move when my phone rang.

"What's going on, *chica?*"

"I called you yesterday. I had the baby this morning."

"Bitch, you lying. I ain't get no call from you."

"Girl, please. I know I called you, but he's here, and he is so precious. You have to see him."

"Where's Alijah at?"

"I have no idea. He left here to run an errand and to get me something to eat and never came back."

"I hate to be the bearer of bad news, but there was a huge bust in Richmond a few hours ago. They said it was a Jamaican dope boy. I heard some friends talking 'bout it. I think it was also on the news, I didn't see it, but he was the first person that popped in my head."

"Are you fucking serious? Do you know where they had the bust at? Oh my fucking God." I bust out crying.

My tears turned into rage as I screamed as loud as I did when I gave birth to Azir. This cannot possibly be happening. Not now, not ever. He was just getting ready to leave the game alone. We were leaving. The nurse must've heard the commotion because she came in to check on me.

"I heard you screaming. Is there anything that I can help you with?"

"No, I'm fine," I told her and put my head under the cover. I was shaking uncontrollably.

I needed to find my man. I did not want to believe what Mo' said, but there was something inside me telling me that she was right. There was no way he would have left me and his son up in the hospital for all those damn hours without calling or coming back to check on us.

Mo' stayed on the phone while I cried.

"Sierra, visiting hours are over, but I'll be there first thing in the morning. I'll also make some calls to see if it's them. I love you, girl. Just be strong for you and my god-baby."

I hung the phone up without responding. I then dialed Jeanette's number to check if she'd seen the news. She told me she missed the news. I then asked her to go downstairs and check to see if his truck was gone. It was gone, so he was driving it.

"Sierra, what's going on? Is Alijah in trouble?"

"Not sure what's going on; just trying to get in touch with him," I said and hung up before she could respond with a hundred questions that I obviously had no answers to. I remembered that I had Saleem's number from the last time, so I scrolled down and found it. I dialed his number, and it just rang until the voice mail picked up. Shit was starting to seem more real by the minute.

It was time to feed and change my baby, so I got up and handled that. I knew he was a newborn, so even though I was hurting, I kept a smile on my face while I fed him. I was scared that he might sense that his mommy was hurting and daddy might be in trouble. I had to protect him, no matter at what cost.

He went back to sleep, and I cried myself to sleep and only woke up at 6:00 a.m. when the nurse came in to take my vitals. She also helped me to get to the bathroom to freshen up. I was happy that I was able to get a little rest in, because I was running off air. After I got all that out of the way, I cut the television on to catch the morning news. Mo' mentioned it made the news so more than likely, it would come on the morning news also.

I paid no attention about other stories that the news anchor was reporting. I looked up when I heard her mention *"Federal authorities broke up a major drug ring in the Commonwealth that stretched from Jamaica, Miami, New York, and Virginia. Three suspects are in custody as they were arrested when authorities came upon a hit that was supposed to be carried out on the wife of one of the suspects. We are going through the charges and will be in touch with the U.S. attorney's office and will bring you more on this major crime enterprise. Lori Gamble reporting for WTVR Richmond, Virginia."* I stared ahead at the television as I saw Alijah, Chuck, and Dre's faces staring back at me through the television screen.

I cut the television off and threw the remote at the wall, breaking it and putting a dent into the thin hospital Sheetrock. I wanted to scream out, but I couldn't. I just sat there crying in silence.

I needed to know where they're holding him so I could get a lawyer down there fast. I had the number for the lawyer from the previous case, so I definitely was going to call him. It was a little too early, but fuck it. I was up, so everybody else needed to get their asses up too. I dialed his number but got no response. I left him a voice mail, giving him the little details that I knew and also letting him know how urgent it was for him to get back with me. I hope he checked his messages soon because I needed his Johnny Cochran-wannabe ass to get on this immediately.

Next, I pushed the call button for the nurse. I needed to know what time the doctor was coming in. I have to get up out of here. I couldn't sit around, not knowing what the fuck went down and how it all played out. I definitely need to talk to him. I learned that the doctor would be in at 9:00 a.m., which was great news to me because I couldn't be of any help here in the hospital.

My baby kept crying, so I got up and walked him around the room, trying to sing to him, but that was not helping at all. I finally called for the nurse. I explained to her that he wouldn't stop crying and I thought something was wrong. She came and explained to me that it wasn't a big deal; newborns sometimes get fussy from a stomachache. She decided to take him to the nursery to give me a little break. I appreciated that.

The doctor finally walked in, a big smile on his face. He congratulated me on the birth and also discharged me. I was in another zone. Nothing he was saying to me was registering. I just needed to get the fuck up out of here so I could go check on my man.

Shayna Jackson

The wait took forever. I didn't like to be around all these law enforcement people. Even though we had a common interest, I still did not like them. They used people to get whatever the hell that they wanted.

One of the agents got word that the suspects were entering the room. I knew Alijah was dumb; just never thought he would have walked up in there like that. He actually thought killing me would be that easy. I see Mr. Jackson still had some things to learn. What those lames used to say fit, "You can't play a player." Oh well, I guess his black ass just got played!

"We got him! We got the suspect Alijah Jackson in custody."

"Yes, the operation went smoothly without incident," the younger agent bragged.

I turned around and smiled at them. I was filled with joy, after years and years of dealing with his ass. His cheating ways and his disrespect toward me—it was finally over. He really thought he was above the law—above everything because he had money. One thing I know about the feds, though; they have an eight-digit number for that ass, and it did not matter how much money you had. As for the last census the Bureau of Prisons had, the feds had a 99-percent conviction rate, and I doubt Alijah will be in the lucky 1 percent.

I knew it wasn't totally over; in fact, it was only the beginning. Part of the deal with the feds was that I had to testify against him. This was going to be my biggest role in life. Mr. Jackson was going to regret the day that he ever crossed Mrs. Jackson.

I heard all the commotion out in the hallway and wanted to be nosy, but they prevented me from going anywhere close to the peephole. I just know there was a lot of yelling going on. I knew Alijah's ass had to be in shock when he realized that he'd been tricked like a cheap slut.

Chapter Fourteen

Alijah Jackson

They took us to the Richmond city jail, claiming they were housing us there until our court appearance; then we would be transferred to a federal holding facility. I was booked and placed in G2, the same cell block where I was housed when I was there the last time. I was separated from my niggas. My old celly from last time was no longer there, and I noticed there was a bunch of little young niggas housed on this tier. I made a mental note to stay out of the way.

I didn't use the phone when I was in booking. Truth was, I did not know what to say to Sierra. Had no idea how to explain to her that I managed to get myself locked up on what was supposed to be the most important day of our lives: the birth of our son. I didn't show it, but I was hurting in the worst way. Hours ago, I was witnessing the birth of my little man. I felt proud knowing that

I played a major role in his existence. Shit was so fucked up, and I had to figure out what my next move was going to be.

I barely got a chance to step foot on the tier when I heard my name being called for an attorney visit. That was definitely fast; at least now I could really get a proper insight of what just took place. I also knew that Sierra got word about my arrest, and she was on her job, as usual.

I walked through the hallway up to the attorney room. I peeped dude sitting down with a pile of papers on the table. He stood up as I approached the table.

"Alijah, my man," he said, shaking my hand.

"Whaddup, son?"

"Sit down; we have things to get to."

"Bet." I was eager to hear what he had to say.

"All right, Ms. Rogers called and told me that you were locked up, so I jumped right on it. You are being charged with some serious offenses, over thirty counts of murder and drug charges. The federal government is going after you hard."

"What the fuck! This dude I had on my team was a fucking undercover agent."

"This is the reason why I said that you are in deep shit, pardon my French. Just by looking at your charges on the indictment, I say they have a lot of ammunition against you."

"Man, I want to kill that nigga and that bitch!"

"I assume you are talking about your wife. They claimed the botched murder plot on her life."

"Yea, that's what they say. I should've killed that stanking-ass bitch years ago."

"Well, I'm happy you didn't."

"Fuck all that; find me a fucking hit man so I can dead this ho!" I shouted.

"You know I can't do that! What I *can* do and *will* do is provide you with the best defense possible. I want to let you know, though, we have our work cut out for us, and we goin' have to fight our ass off to get some of these charges dropped or reduced. The feds are not easy to beat, but I'm ready."

"Man, when you get outta here, holla at Sierra. Tell her I said to throw you some paper to cover my niggas' lawyer fees."

"Okay, I gotcha. I'm also going to bring in two other lawyers from my firm on the case, and also a private investigator that will be working on gathering everything on the two witnesses in the case. I need to discredit them, so I need everything from the day they were born to now."

"A'ight, cool. So what's the next move?"

"You will be going up for a bond hearing, which I doubt will be granted. The arraignment is up next; that'll be about a week or two. You will be formally charged, and you plead not guilty. I will then put in a motion for discovery to get all the evidence against you. Oh, and I will also put in a motion for a speedy trial. Earlier, I spoke to the U.S. attorney on your case, and she disclosed that they have recorded phone conversations, so I put in the motion to get those so I can listen to them, and we can go from there."

That right there blew me. I know most of my shit was handled on the phone. The more I listened to all the evidence they claimed they had against me, the farther I saw my life slipping away from me. I tried to stay calm, but deep down, I was fuming with so much anger. I could kill a nigga with my bare hands. I saw no light at the end of all the darkness. None!

"One more thing . . . When you talk to Sierra, makes sure you tell her to keep the house clean and to keep her circle tight."

"Okay, I gotcha!"

I knew Sierra was not charged, but I wasn't sure if her name was involved. I know how the feds play dirty, and they might get at her to put pressure on me. I wasn't worried about the phone conversation between the two of us. The phone that we talked on was a private number that only the two of us knew about, and every week, I changed phones and got new numbers. As far as anything else, I have always kept her out of it, in fear of this exact situation presenting itself.

We rapped a little longer, and then he left. I made my way back to the pod and made my first phone call to Sierra. I might as well go ahead and face her now.

Sierra Rogers

Li'l Mo' showed up just in time. I was ready to get the hell on. My car was in the parking lot, but I was in no shape to drive home. I decide to let it stay parked and ride home with Mo'. I would come back and get the car at a later date.

I dressed Azir in one of his cute Rocawear snowsuits and placed him in the car seat. I thanked all the nurses and then sat in the wheelchair as the nurse's aide pushed me out the door. Mo' carried the car seat, and we loaded up in her car.

"Hey, boo, how you feeling?"

"Terrible. It was Alijah and his boys that got locked up."

"Damn, how you know?"

"I saw them on the news this morning."

"Wow! That's crazy."

"I know. I don't know what the fuck's going on. I just need to get home so I can sort all this shit out."

"Well, I'll be there. I know me and him had our falling out, but I know how you feel about him, so I'm going to be there for you."

"Thanks, girl. For a minute, I thought that you wasn't fuckin' wit' me, but I see you still my bitch."

"Girl, I was tight at that nigga for disrespecting me, and I needed some time away. But we been through too much to let a nigga come between us; you feel me?"

I was happy to hear those words, because I needed a friend. My heart was broken, and I didn't know how I was going to survive. I felt like I wanted to die!

We pulled up at the house and got out of the car. Jeanette was waiting for us downstairs.

"Come here, little man. Nana is going to spoil you."

I saw the surprised look on Mo's face. She knew the full story of Jeanette abandoning me. So this came as a surprise to her, but I didn't feel like I had to keep explaining my reasons why I decided to let her back in my life. I knew she wasn't no role model, and I didn't expect anyone to understand where I was coming from. I just know that after I got shot, I realized that life was too short, and I didn't want to have any regrets.

Jeanette took Azir upstairs while Mo' and I stayed in the living room. It was time for me to get to the bottom of everything.

The lawyer finally called, and as you can imagine, I was furious at his black ass. I left him a message, hours ago, and this fool claimed he was tied up. Like I give a fuck. I told him about Alijah's situation and told him I need him on the case ASAP. I decided to meet him the next day with a check. I was so upset with him I hung the phone up without even saying good-bye.

Mo' and I talked for a little longer.

"Sierra, you need to put something on your stomach," Mo' said.

"I can't right now. I need to know where they holding him and his first court appearance."

"Trust me, I understand. That's how I felt when Troy got torn off. But you just had a baby and you're bleeding, so you need to put something on your stomach."

"OK, Mo', I hear you," I said in an annoyed tone. That was my cue for her to shut the hell up.

We sat a little longer; then she bounced.

***

Jeanette bathed Azir and fed him, then put him to sleep. After that, she joined me in the living room. She sat on the sofa beside me.

"I won't ask how you feeling. That would be a stupid question, but, baby, you need to be strong. Alijah need you more than ever now. You have to be his voice on this side of the fence."

"Hmm . . . Strong for him? I can't even be strong for my own damn self. I can't do this. He was getting ready to walk away from the game. All he wanted was his family; he wants to be in his son's life. I dreaded this was going to happen."

"Sierra, this is only man's law. God has the last say; don't give up on him coming home so fast. Hold the faith and fight for your family."

I needed her to shut the fuck up with this damn preaching that ain't going to change a damn thing or bring my man home. She got the drift and headed on back upstairs. I was eager to get the call from the attorney. I was tempted to blow up his phone. Instead, I decided to wait a little longer. I called the Richmond City Jail and found out they had him, and he was waiting to be transferred. The bitch at the desk would not give me any more information.

I felt helpless. I recalled the last time when he got locked up, I was able to set the faggot up and had the case dropped. Lord knew I was in over my head. Everybody knew that the feds ain't the ones to play with. I have never heard of one nigga that beat them before, and the numbers that they gave out was nothing nice. My thoughts were interrupted by the ringing of my cell phone.

"Hello."

"OK, Ms. Rogers, I located Mr. Jackson, and I went to see him. This is where we stand; it was a sting operation at the Marriott Hotel. Mr. Jackson and his boys were also set up by an undercover agent that was a part of his crew. He's being charged with multiple counts of murders, drug trafficking, and money laundering. I have to tell you, these are some serious charges."

"All right, I hear you. So what's the bottom line?"

"Well, he will go in front of the judge for a bond hearing; then we will go from there. I tell you from what I have already seen, the case is a tough one, but I will give it my best shot."

"What the hell you mean? You better get in there and *fight* for my man like it's *your* life. I need him home!" I yelled in the phone.

"Ms. Rogers, believe me, I understand your frustrations. His bail hearing is in the morning at the Federal Courthouse on Broad at

10:00 a.m. I'm pretty sure he wants to see you, and we can talk after court."

"Sure, I'll see you then." I hung the phone up.

I shouldn't be going off on the attorney, but I was pissed off. I wasn't going to sit and pretend that shit was good, because it wasn't. I needed a drink and a blunt bad. I had an idea where Alijah kept his stash, so I went into it and took out some weed. I rolled me a blunt and poured a glass of Baileys. It didn't matter any that I just came home from the hospital. I needed something to numb my pain.

I heard Jeanette's footsteps coming down the stairs, but I continued on doing me.

"Sierra, are you drinking and smoking? You just had a baby, and you're on medication."

"Who the hell you talking to? I'm grown as fuck! Don't you ever try to check me in my fucking house, or you can get the hell on."

"I know you're hurting, but this is not the right way to go about it. You can have a bad reaction mixing your medication with alcohol."

"And this warning is coming from a person that used crack, mixed it with weed, sniffed powder, and shot heroin, all at the same damn time. Ha-ha, you are hilarious."

She didn't respond. She just stood there and shook her head at me. A moment later, she walked off. I was going to scream at her again; instead, I just puffed some more of the high-grade herb and sipped on my drink. Fuck whoever wanted to judge me. I would answer to God when it's my time. Until then, I was going to do whatever the hell I wanted to do and see who was going to check me.

I woke up with a hangover and a terrible headache. That was the only thing that I didn't like about drinking. I took some Tylenol and walked upstairs to check on my baby. My intention last night was to go upstairs after I was finished, but that didn't happen.

I knocked on Jeanette's door to get my baby.

"Come in."

"Hey, Mommy's bundle of joy." I picked him up off the bed.

"Chile, he been up all night. He reminds me of you; slept all day and stayed up at night."

"Is that right, li'l man? You gave Nana a hard time?" I said while tickling him.

"Listen, Jeanette, I apologize 'bout last night. I was out of place. I had no business trying to tell you how to live your life."

"OK."

I left it at that; I wasn't in the mood to debate. My head was killing me, and I had to be in court.

"I have to go to court around ten. If you don't mind, can you watch Azir for me?"

"Of course. Just go ahead get yourself together and go see 'bout that boy's daddy."

I turned around to tell her how much I appreciated her. The words never came out, so I turned back around again and left the room.

I took a hot shower; this was my first real bath since I had Azir, and as always, the water does the body good. I still wasn't feeling like my old self, but I had things to tend to. I got dressed and was ready to tackle all this chaos. I needed money for the lawyer, so I went downstairs to the safe that Alijah built in the house. I used the code that he gave me months ago; I never had a reason to go in there until now. The safe popped open, and my heart skipped a beat. I have *never* seen so much cash in my life before. There were stacks upon stacks. I felt nervous just standing there. I looked around to make sure no one was spying on me. I knew he was grinding, but I had no idea that he was caked up like that. I counted out a hundred grand and closed it up. I wasn't sure about the lawyer fee, so I took out enough to pay for his fee and his boys. If it wasn't enough, then I would get more.

I put the money in the biggest bag that I owned. I see now the reason why he always told me that if anything ever happened to him, we'd be set for life. I locked the basement door and checked it twice. Then I went upstairs, kissed the baby, and left.

I didn't realize that my car was still parked in the hospital parking lot until I got in the garage and saw it was not there. I had no choice but to drive Alijah's Lexus. I got his spare key and hit the road. His car was faster than mine, but I was a pro, so it came natural to maneuver it.

His bail hearing was at ten o' clock. I checked my phone. It was around that time. I parked and placed the bag of money in my trunk. I locked it with hopes that nobody would fuck with my car while I was gone. I decided not to carry the money with me because I was going up in the federal building where security was tight, and I didn't want to get noticed with all that money.

I went through security and showed my identification. His lawyer was already there, so I went over to talk to him. He told me he was going to go for a bond, but it might not happen. Before we could continue with our conversation, the judge and the U.S. attorney entered the courtroom.

The marshals brought in Chuck first, followed by Dre and Alijah. They were chained around the waist to their ankles. These motherfuckers were not playing any games; they really thought that they were killers. Alijah and I glanced at each other. He smiled at me, and I whispered, "I love you" to him.

The procedure was the same as any other bail hearing. The U.S. attorney called the undercover agent to the stand where he testified about all the crimes that he witnessed. Remind you this was the same dude that Alijah brought on his team after Darryl got killed. I was furious when I saw that nigga's face. Sitting there listening to everything dude was saying, I knew Alijah's future didn't look too bright. This dude knew too much about the business. I didn't see him the day that I called Alijah to help me, but does that mean he didn't know? I couldn't think straight.

I wanted to leave, but I had to stay. I need to hear everything for myself. However, I couldn't focus; I sat there numb and spaced out. I hardly heard anything either side was arguing about. All I heard was mumbling between them. I sat up and tried to pay attention. I saw when only the district attorney took the stand. I did not expect him to be there. Fuck that, I never thought that I would ever see him after our last encounter. He looked at me and smiled. I did not think anything was funny.

I sat there while he testified. I wish I wasn't here. I was so caught up in Alijah's drama, totally ignoring the fact that last year I set that faggot up, and three days ago, I murdered my ex-best friend. Reality quickly set in, and I knew at that point, I needed to hire my own defense attorney.

Alijah's attorney tried to paint him as a family man. He even mentioned that just days ago he became a dad. None of that effort was any match for the evidence that the government put on, describing Alijah as a cold-blooded murderer; a drug kingpin who has ties to Jamaica, England, and the Cayman Islands. The way he painted him, he was nothing short of a monster. After listening to both sides, the judge denied bond.

I saw the lawyer whispering to Alijah before they led him out. This time he did not look at me because if he did, he would've seen the long tears rolling down my face. I stood there until they led him out of sight behind the huge double doors.

Then I got up and proceeded to walk out. I had my head lowered until I bumped into someone. I was getting ready to say excuse me until I picked my head up and realized who was standing in front of me.

"Well, well, well. Hello, Ms. Williams. Or should I say Sierra Rogers? I see we meet again."

"What the hell you want? I thought we had a deal."

"Ha-ha. A fucking deal? You fucking walked into my life and set me up with your little friend, then had the nerve to blackmail me. Here you are talking about a frigging deal."

"Listen to me, you faggot! I still have a copy of the tape. Trust me, I won't think twice to send it to Channel 6 news," I spat.

"Lord, you must have not seen the news the other day. I made a public announcement that I was leaving my wife for my man. Honey, you are so late."

I was definitely caught off guard, but I wasn't about to let that clown see me sweat.

"You are fucking disgusting. Stay the hell away from me."

"Ms. Rogers, I feel pity for you. I thought about charging your ass with blackmail, but decided you're a waste of human life. Plus, I did like the way your friend sucked my dick. Woiee, Lord, he sure know how to suck a cock," he bragged.

I couldn't stand there and listen to that nastiness. I pushed him out of the way and stepped into the hallway. I was already upset, and then that clown just completely blew me. I was ready to go home, but I needed to talk to the attorney.

He was still in the courthouse talking with the feds. It was another twenty minutes before he came out.

"Sorry to keep you waiting. I just needed to see which direction they're heading with the case."

"No sweat. I have the money in my car. We can walk and talk."

"As you have heard, there is no bond. The next step will be his arraignment. That's when he will be formally charged. We will plead not guilty. I put in a motion for discovery so I can know all the evidence they have on him."

"So what are the chances of him beating these charges?"

"Realistically? I say just from browsing through all the evidence they claim that they have, I can't really draw a conclusion. I promise you, though, I will fight for him until I can't fight anymore."

"I need an attorney."

"Are you in trouble?"

"Nah, at least not yet. I just don't know if they might come after me because I'm his woman."

"I doubt it. You have your own business and money, but with the feds you never know. I have a partner in the firm. He's very experienced. I'll put him in touch with you."

"I appreciate that. So when are they moving him?"

"This afternoon they will be transporting him to Northern Neck Regional Jail in Warsaw. That's about a forty-five-minute drive from Richmond. You might want to call them and get their visiting hours. I'll be up there soon as I get all the information that I need."

I popped the trunk and gave him the money.

"Here's a hundred grand. Let me know if you need more. I don't care how much it costs to get him the best possible defense, and I heard you are one of the best, so please help him."

"Thank you. I will put this toward all three of their legal defenses. Alijah is stronger than you think. He is more worried about you and the baby."

"Well, we're going to be a'ight. We just need him home with us."

"Absolutely! I have to run. I have another client to meet up with. You have my number; ring me if you need anything."

"Alrighty then."

I watched as he clutched his briefcase close to him and walked in the opposite direction. I got into my car and headed home.

Chapter Fifteen

Sierra Rogers

I was feeling tired, mentally and physically drained. I had no idea when things were going to get better. They said to be careful of what you ask for, and that statement has proved to be true. I recall growing up in Creighton, and all I ever dreamed of was meeting a rich dope boy and moving out of the projects. I didn't bargain for all the bullshit that came with it. I mean, ever since we started our lives together, it's been chaos, even to the point where I could've lost my life. "Why was I this unlucky? What did I do wrong?" I asked myself.

After sitting in court and hearing all the charges that were brought against Alijah, I couldn't help but to feel a little down. I knew I had to stay optimistic for him and my son, but I felt like there's no way out this time. Tears rolled down my face as the severe heartache took its toll on my fragile heart.

I pulled in my driveway and tiptoed upstairs. I needed a minute to myself, just one minute to lie down and cry. I need God to take all the pain away. It was times like this I would really love to hear my grandma's voice or feel her tender touch. I lay in my bed crying, thinking she'd appear like she usually did. Seconds turn into minutes, minutes into hours, and still, nothing happened.

Then the cell phone rang and woke me out of my daze. I jumped up and answered it.

"You have a prepaid call. You will not be charged for this call. Press five to speak." My fingers trembled as I pressed five to accept the call.

"Hello," I barely manage to say.

"Whaddup, ma? Why you sound like that?"

"Hey, boo, how you holding up?"

"I'm here, you know, but I don't like how you sound."

I couldn't hold it any longer. I bust out bawling.

"Sierra, baby, don't do that. You are tearing me down right now."

I couldn't stop the flow of tears that had built up in me. I just held the phone next to my ear as he expressed his love for his son and me, words that seemed empty. I need more than words.

I need him to hold me, for him to tell me that it was only a bad dream. I waited to hear those words, but they never came.

"Sierra, dry them tears. The phone is about to hang up, and they gonna move me to Warsaw. Bring li'l man to see me. I love you, baby girl."

The call disconnected before I got a chance to tell him I love him. It was nice to hear his voice, but I wish I would've talked more. He has no idea the hurt he placed on me. I wish I could've just walked away from him and the nightmare, but I couldn't. My heart wouldn't let me; instead, it kept me hostage, bound to a life that has nothing but unhappy endings.

Jeanette had really stepped up to be the support that I needed. The last few days she's been helping out with Azir. I never thought that when I asked her to come live with me she would turn out to be a rock for me. I can honestly say our relationship has been improving over time.

I spoke to my lawyer; he seems like a nice guy. I wasn't charged with any crime, so there was no need for him. I just need him on standby, just in case anything jumped off. He also informed me that the feds might be snooping into Alijah's affairs, and because I was his woman, I might become a target of their investigation. He even implied that they might place me under surveillance, and they might also have our phone calls recorded. I rolled my eyes while he was telling me these things. I was not a stranger to dope boys or the law. I knew they played dirty, and I was ready for them. One thing about it, Creighton didn't raise no fool, and I damn sure wasn't going to roll over on my man.

It was Monday, and I was getting ready to visit Alijah. I got Azir dressed, and we were out the door to see his daddy. This was a special day because this was Alijah's first day seeing his son since he cut the umbilical cord. We definitely had to make a grand appearance. I like to look my best, even when I was feeling shitty. I was looking damn good, and I was happy that I did not lose my ass, which was my signature. I smiled as I thought that was the same ass that caught Alijah's attention in the first place.

Mo' had picked my car up from the hospital the other day so I didn't have to drive Alijah's car. I love my BMW. It's like we done bonded so much; plus, my baby bought it for me, so it had sentimental meanings.

I was born and raised in Richmond, and this was my first time crossing over the Tappahannock Bridge, and, damn, it was different scenery. I could tell it was an old hick town with horses and cows. I had no understanding why they would put a bunch of inmates in a town like that when the majority are blacks.

I've always heard horror stories about blacks getting pulled over by the white racist police, so I maintained the speed limit and drove carefully to the jail. It was a five-minute wait before visitation hours.

My name was called, and I walked to the area where Alijah waited. A glass separated us, and we conversed by a telephone.

"Hey, honey."

"Whaddup, sweetheart? You look beautiful, and my little man is growing. Turn him around so I can see his face."

I turned Azir around to face his daddy. He was wide awake, bobbing his head from side to side. I saw the joy that was plastered across Alijah's face as he smiled and spit baby talk to his one and only child. I was beginning to tear up, but I used my inner strength to stop it from coming and making an appearance.

"So, baby girl, how you holding up?"

"Not good at all. It's like I keep telling myself that it's only a dream, and I am going to wake up," I said while I sadly shook my head.

"Ma, I wish that I could tell you that, but the truth is, it's real as fuck. I saw the lawyer yesterday, and things didn't look too good. I don't even know how it's going to turn out."

I sighed. "Alijah, we have to fight, baby. We have to. I am not giving up. I just can't."

"Sierra, listen to me. I love myself, but I love y'all more. Shit is bad, straight up. You need to get e'erything and move on, you and li'l man."

"What the hell are you saying? You didn't even go to trial yet, and you already giving up?"

"That's not what I'm saying, B. All I'm saying is I don't live in a fantasy world, and I don't want you to either. You need to prepare yourself for whatever these crackers might throw at me. You feel me?"

I stood there holding our son, and this nigga is telling me to prepare myself, because he might be gone for good. I don't know how I was supposed to really feel about that, so I just let the tears flow.

"Ma, I ain't tryna hurt your feelings or anything like that. Trust me, I wish on e'erything I love that I could take away all your hurt, but right 'bout now, I can't do shit!"

I stood there frozen, without uttering a word. I just stared at him, and then looked at my son. I wondered if he knew what the fuck he was saying to me. Obviously, he didn't.

"Baby girl, I love you with e'erything in me. You the first chick that ever made a nigga shed tears, and seeing you cry right now is killing me. And the fucked-up part is I can't even hold you or my seed. B, I need you to know, no matter how this play out, you and my seed is good for life. I made sure of that."

"We will *never* be good without you. You are our family; shit will never be the same. I fucking *need* you. My son *needs* his daddy," I cried out, not giving a damn who might've heard me.

I saw the tears drop from his eyes. I could tell he was fighting to not let them flow. I could not imagine what pain he was feeling. I stood there in silence, because honestly, I was at a loss for words. I wanted to hold him in my arms, to let him know we are in this together. I held my tears back. The fact was, I did not know what he was going through.

"Ma, listen, visitation is almost over, but real quick, make sure you clean up the house. You know you don't like no dirty house, and make sure you get *all* the dirt out of the corners."

"OK," I whispered.

"I love you. Yo, be safe out there and kiss my li'l man for me and make sure you let him know that his daddy loves him. I love you too, shorty. Don't you ever doubt that."

I saw the guard motioning for him to hang up the phone and another one yelling, "Visitations are over."

"I love you, boo, and I ain't going anywhere. I will be right here waiting on you."

The guard led him and the other inmates out of the room. I wrapped my baby in his blanket and walked out to my car.

I knew Alijah was trying to tell me something when he told me to clean up. I didn't fully understand him, and the only thing that came to mind was the money that was downstairs. All the guns were gone. *Hmm.* I intend to do a thorough search of the entire house *and* his car. I placed Azir into his car seat and drove out of the jail parking lot. It looked like it was going to snow, so I need to head home before the streets get covered.

I got home safe and sound. Jeanette was in the kitchen cooking dinner.

"Hey."

"Hey, honey, you look beat, and my sugar pooh looks cold. Let me wash my hands and take him."

I sat on the stool in the kitchen. She had no idea how worn-out I was feeling. I was happy that I saw Alijah. I wasn't happy knowing that he might not be coming home. She washed her hands and took Azir out of my lap. I am not going to front, having her around really lifted some of the burden off me.

"How was your visit?"

"It was OK, nothing special. Azir got to see his daddy."

"I hope I'm not prying, but how is he holding up?"

"He a'ight, but seems to me like he's giving up. I really don't know."

I didn't want to discuss it. The fact is people always pretend like they know what you're going through, but they really don't know unless they were in the same boat.

"I'm praying for him and for you and Azir. God has a way to show up and show out when we least expect him."

"Yea, well, where he at right now? 'Cause I sure do need him," I replied sarcastically.

"I know you don't want to hear this, but he sees and knows all things and will never forsake his children."

"OK, I hear you; however, I am not in the mood right now for church. I'm going upstairs; bring me my baby when you're ready."

I picked up my purse and strolled upstairs. I believe in God, but my faith was really slim to none at the time. I changed into something comfortable, then got into my bed. I cut on the television and turned it to the Discovery Channel. I didn't want to watch the news or any detective shows with people getting locked up. My own life was too dramatic.

I cut my phone off, not that I did not want to talk to Alijah or anyone else. I just needed some time to myself. I've been thinking for days that I need to settle the score with the next bitch on my list. See, I fully understood that she was angry because I took her husband, but let's recap; her man came checking for me, and in the beginning, I was an innocent party. I never knew he was married, and when I did find out, I was already in love with him. I owe that bitch no explanations; we weren't friends. She was just a random bitch to me. It was all game until she crossed her boundaries and tried to kill me.

This bitch thought shit was sweet. She was still running around causing trouble in our lives.

That ho didn't know, but ever since I woke up in the hospital, not a day has gone by that I don't sit and think about her and the different ways I wanted to kill her. I wanted to see the bitch bleed until she's taken that last breath. The only thing that was slowing me down was the fact that she was a federal informant, and that meant the feds might be protecting that ass. So I had to view the options that were available to me and go from there. I had to be very careful because I didn't want to get caught up the way they set up Alijah and his boys.

I really wish I could've left it alone, but I couldn't. Those two bitches violated me, and I've already dealt with Neisha's ass. Now it was Shayna's turn. First, I need to find that bitch; then I can put my plan into motion.

Jeanette interrupted my thoughts when she came into the room and handed me a cup of ginger tea.

"Are you going to eat dinner?"

"Nah, I'm not hungry. Cover it up for me. I'll eat it tomorrow."

"Sierra, you need to eat. You just had a baby; you need to nurse your body back to health."

"Jeanette, lemme ask you a question. How come you know all what's good for me now, but you didn't when I was younger?"

"Sierra, you are hurting, and you're looking to pick a fight. I won't be no part of it. Get some rest and holler if you need me. Azir is already asleep," she said and exited the room.

I threw the cup of tea onto the wall, breaking the cup.

"Fuck you. I need answers, but instead, you run off like you did before. Fuck you." I grabbed my pillow and bit down into it. I *was* hurting. I felt like all the walls around me was crumbling down. I need air; I need to breathe. I cried harder with snot all over the place. I didn't care. My head was pounding, but that was no pain when compared to my broken heart.

Chapter Sixteen

Alijah Jackson

I haven't slept one good night since I been on lock. My days were spent exercising or chopping it up with the li'l homie from BK. He seemed pretty cool and was locked up for numerous bodies in Alexandria. My nights were the worst. I would do push-ups until I was hurting. Then I would lie on the bunk, just mainly brainstorming.

I missed my son terribly; it was breaking me down, literally. I tried my best not to focus on what was going to happen; instead, I tried to picture me teaching him how to kick a ball, how to ride a bike. These are the things that only a father should be able to teach his firstborn.

I often thought about Mom-dukes. I've been dreading on making that phone call to her because it was going to hurt her something serious. I still could hear her voice in my head warning me to leave those streets alone. I don't have the words to soothe her wounds or to begin to explain why I chose these streets. I just hope one day she will understand that this was the life I chose, and there are only two outcomes.

It was a new day but the same shit. It ain't too much to do when you locked up. I called Sierra, and we talked. She was excited about going back to work. She informed me she was going to hire a babysitter for Azir. I wasn't feeling that bullshit, but look where I was. How can I even try to run shit from the inside? I made sure I told her to check that bitch out thoroughly and to make sure she stayed on top of e'erything. Sierra was on some foul shit for real 'cause she had money to take care of both of them, but yet, she's talking about running a fucking shop. I had a feeling that chickenhead bitch Mo' had a hand in her making that decision. By the time our call ended, she knew I was tight as fuck.

It was mail call, and I wasn't expecting any letters. I just got cards from Sierra yesterday, and she was the only one that wrote me. I sat by the table playing cards with the homie when I heard the CO call my name. I got up and walked hastily over to him. I then realized it was legal mail that I had to sign my name on in order to get it. I signed, and the CO handed me a large manila envelope. I took it and marched into my cell. Those niggas were nosy as fuck, but I wasn't no fool to let these snitch-ass niggas all up in my BI.

I ripped the envelope open. The top page said "*Motion of Discovery*." I felt anxious and tight at the same damn time. I needed to know, so I started to read the document. Line by line they detailed crimes going back to my younger days in New York, the Creighton murders—and then I stopped dead in my tracks when I read the murder of Markus. The reason why that grabbed my full attention was because the day that I merked that nigga, I only made one phone call, and that was to my big homie, Saleem. So how the fuck would they have all the details about it? I kept on reading. The murder of Shayna's parents was also in there. I was also being charged as a drug kingpin and the mastermind behind numerous murders.

As if shit couldn't get any worse—I got to the part where they named the informants: Agent Damion Somers, Shayna Jackson, and . . . *Adrienne Coleman!*

"Get the fuck outta here!" I yelled out. "What? Big homie is an undercover agent?"

There's no fucking way that was possible. I got up off the bed, which was a mistake because the room started to spin. I became light-headed; it felt like a sharp sword just pierced my heart. This was not anger that I was feeling—it was straight hardcore pain.

I took my mind back to the first time we met. He used to be posted outside the Islamic Center on 125th. Whenever Darryl and I walked by, he would speak to us. After a while, we became cool and started hanging tight. That's when I learned that he was moving major weight. I wondered when the fuck did he become an agent or was he always an agent that was planted among dealers. I can't even wrap my mind around the idea. I've been dealing with this man for over *ten* fucking years!

"Yo' what the rass a happen, Father God? Jah know star, a fuckery dis."

This fucking case couldn't get any worse. Something else also hit me . . . He was not present at my bond hearing, and that alone seemed weird. I also remember my homie telling me that the feds mentioned his name when they were in the hotel. I couldn't stand to read anymore, so I put the document under my mattress.

I sat there pondering . . . ten years of friendship or was it ten years of him reeling me in to gain my trust? I let this nigga in my life and not just that—he knew *every* inch of my business. He was the main drive behind me moving to VA. I now see that it was all a setup. I've been played and fucked straight like a bitch. I lay on my bunk staring at the light. There wasn't one thought that could've shed any type of light on the fuckery that was taking place.

The next morning was here, and I had a lawyer visit. Didn't see the use of the visit 'cause I see the deck was stacked against me. Father God was my only hope in all this chaos. I walked into the visitation room where my lawyer was seated.

"Whaddup, yo?" I asked as I sat across from him.

"How are you holding up?"

"I'm livin'."

"Great! Let's get down to business. I take it you already received your motion to discovery. What I sent you is only the tip of the iceberg. There are hours upon hours of wiretapping. My partner and I are taking turns listening to the recordings. There is damaging evidence in there. Each time Agent Coleman and Somers conversed with you, it was recorded."

I sat there with my head buried in my hands.

"So, you the lawyer. What are my chances of beating these charges?"

"Tsk . . . I say zero to none. My best advice to you would be for you to plead out before any of the other guys do, and we probably can get time off for cooperating with the feds."

I stood up and shoved the chair toward him.

"Yo! What the fuck you implying? You tryna tell me that I should become a fucking rat?"

"Calm down. As your attorney, I'm just pointing out your best possible options. These are some serious charges, and you are facing life in prison."

"I don't give a fuck. Mi is a bad man and mi nah tun no snitch. I ride for my niggas all pussyclaat day. Trust mi on that."

"I hear you, but I don't believe you understand how serious this is. We can go to trial, and if we lose, you will get multiple life sentences."

I took a few steps closer to that clown and grabbed him by his collar. "Listen up, pussy hole. I will *never* become a rat. I am not pleading out. I am going to trial, and if you can't do your fucking job, lemme know so I can get a nigga that don't mind fighting for me. Son, you feel me?"

"Alijah, you're the boss. You want to go to trial, so that's what we are going to do. I need everything that you know about Somers, Coleman, and your wife. They are going to testify, so I need to know every little detail about them."

"Man, whatever the fuck you say. I'm out!" I turned to leave.

"Mr. Jackson . . ."

I heard the fool hollering my name, but I kept on walking. I was over that Johnny Cochran-ass nigga. I can't believe that he suggested that I roll on my niggas. I will die before I ever become a rat. Fuck that; in my world, it was death before dishonor.

I arrived back in my cell and lay down on my bunk. I skipped over lunch and dinner. You can say that I lost my appetite; plus, I needed the time to just kick back and analyze my life. I wonder how I got so reckless and did not see the signs and let these fuck niggas in my life. This was one of those times I wish Darryl were here. I needed my brother more than anything.

I tried to fall asleep, but I couldn't. All I could think about was that I wanted to kill all three of them motherfuckas, nothing rushed. I want to torture them, throw gasoline on them, and then set them on fire. I want them to *feel* my wrath in the extreme.

"Ahhhh!" I screamed out, not giving a fuck that it was lockdown time.

"Jackson, hold that noise down," the fat, white CO shouted at me.

"Nigga, fuck you," I yelled back.

"Watch your mouth. I will throw yo' ass in the hole. This is your last chance," he said and walked off.

"My yute go suck yuh madda," I said.

If this nigga knew what was best for him, he'd keep it moving. I felt homicidal and suicidal, and I was ready to pop off on whoever the fuck wants it.

Chapter Seventeen

Sierra Rogers

The days moved in slow motion. It had only been two weeks since Alijah got locked up, and it felt like two years. We spoke daily on the telephone. That was our only way to keep our love alive. I missed having him around; I missed his laughter and just having him around, period. At times, I open up the closet just to stare at his clothes. I even grab his favorite robe and inhale his masculine scent. I would do anything just to have him home with me.

Our son was steadily growing. He was two weeks old and already started to favor his daddy with those high cheekbones and big brown eyes. The only thing that he took after me was his nose. Jeanette said he resembled me when I was a baby, but what did she know? She was too high back then to remember what I looked like.

Mo' came through, and we hung out in the living room. We smoked two blunts and drank some Alizé. I told her I was ready to come back to work. I was tired of sitting in the house every day. It was driving me insane. Once I go back to work, I'll be busy, and my mind will be occupied. I missed doing hair; it was my passion ever since I was young. I wasn't going to overdo it. I'll start off with two or three days until Azir gets older.

I knocked on Jeanette's door. I have no earthly idea why she kept her door locked, even though it's only the two of us in the house.

"Come in."

"Hey, I need to talk to you about something."

"Sit down." She motioned for me to sit on her bed.

"No, I'm good. I was thinking about going back to the salon for a few days at a time. I was also thinking of hiring a babysitter to help out whenever you have to go to your program."

"Oh, OK. I thought with all that's going on you'd stay home for a while."

"No, I need to keep busy. I don't have Alijah here, so I need to make money and get my independence back."

"I understand where you're coming from. You know I'll help out with him. I don't like no babysitter, but it's your call, chile."

"I'm going to put an ad in the newspaper so I can find somebody. I need references, 'cause God forbid anything happen to my son. I will kill me a bitch."

"Get someone that's experienced with babies, because not everybody have patience with them."

"I got this, trust me. I'll be thorough; I'm not green. This is my first child, but I know how to be careful," I said before I left the room.

For some strange reason, I still felt some kind of way whenever she tries to tell me what she believes to be right. In my mind, I often wonder where she got all this experience from, 'cause it wasn't from being a parent to me.

The next day I placed the ad in the newspaper. I was looking for a female, age thirty-five or older. Three to five years' experience working with newborns. She must have a driver's license and a CPR Certification. I placed my name and contact information so the person can call and set up an interview.

Shayna Jackson

It was weeks, and I still was mourning the loss of my daddy. At times I would stand over his urn which I kept on my dresser. I threw Mama's urn in the closet. She was always so jealous of the relationship between Daddy and me. She used to fuss at him, claiming that he spoiled me. I've never fully understood why she couldn't just allow him to be a good daddy, even if it meant him rubbing my thighs when I would sit on his lap. I even loved when he asked me to kiss "Big Larry" on the tip of the head. See, Daddy and I shared secrets that only we knew about. I wouldn't dare expose them to anyone outside of us. Daddy was gone, and my lips are sealed.

I had a briefing with the feds, and to my surprise, things were moving along smoothly. I was excited because this time, Alijah won't be able to step foot outside of those prison walls. He will be there for the rest of his sick life. Even though I would've preferred the electric chair for him, I'll settle for life imprisonment.

This was the reason why I never trusted the government in the first place. Their asses were two-faced. I already gave them the big man and his crew, but earlier, they informed me that the investigation was not over, and in order for me not to get charged with attempted murder and conspiracy, I had to do one more thing for them. You should've seen my damn face when that Spanish bitch said that.

This bitch just did not know how close I came to slapping off that smirk she walked around with on her face. The only thing that saved her is that she's a United States of America Certified Whore. The bitch went on to tell me what the hell it was that I was supposed to be doing. I busted out laughing midway through her speech. Just a second ago, I wanted to beat that ass, and here I was, seconds later, thinking that bitch was brilliant. I mean, only a bitch of my status could think of such a detailed plan. I hate to admit it, but I loved it.

I was ready for the challenge with my own twist and turns, so I gladly accepted the offer. I left the office, feeling rejuvenated and ready to play the leading role of my lifetime. This was going to be epic; the wife and bottom bitch showdown!

Sierra Rogers

Alijah was arraigned and officially charged with twenty-eight counts of murder and other charges. Basically, they were charging him with being the head nigga in charge. I've heard of niggas being charged with crimes before, but never

that many charges. Common sense told me that
for each count of murder, that was definitely a
life sentence.

A bad feeling filled my stomach, and sour
water gathered in my mouth. I knew that feeling
all too well. I got up and rushed out of the courtroom. I barely made it to the bathroom where I
emptied every bit of food that I consumed earlier
into the toilet. Cold sweat invaded my body as I
knelt on the floor beside the toilet. I was feeling
weak and nauseated. I had to get myself together,
so I stood up slowly and walked over to the sink
and washed my face. I opened my purse and
took out one of the Percocet, which the doctor
prescribed for me, and popped it. I had no idea
how I would've managed if I didn't have those
pills. They've helped me get through the difficult
times. I wiped my face with the paper towel and
dragged myself out of the bathroom.

His case was still in progress. My mind, heart,
and soul couldn't take another second of that
U.S. District Attorney degrading Alijah like he
was the scum of the earth. Obviously, they didn't
know the man. He was my lover, my friend,
and my son's father, and *not* the monster that
they're making him out to be. Finally, I made it
out of the courthouse and got into my car and
returned home.

I had received numerous calls about child care, so I sat on the sofa and called people back one by one. I was down to the last name. This woman left me a message, and the way she sounded, I could tell she was middle-aged. Her voice was soft and warm. I called her, and we set up an appointment for the next morning.

I woke up early and bathed Azir. The little things he does often put a smile on my face and brought me out of my state of darkness. I got dressed and walked downstairs to fix a cup of ginger tea. Jeanette was sitting in the living room watching the news. I made my tea, then joined her in there.

Minutes later, the doorbell rang. I walked over to open the door, but first I peeped through the peephole. I saw a middle-aged woman standing in the cold, so I opened the door to let her in.

"Hello, you must be Ms. Sadie?"

"Yes, yes, and you must be Sierra. Nice to meet you."

I extended my arm and shook her hand.

"Step in, out of the cold."

I walked into the living room with her in pursuit.

"This is Jeanette. She also lives here."

"Hello, nice to meet you," she said, turning to Jeanette.

"Please sit down. Like I said in my ad, I'm looking for a babysitter for my son. He's six weeks old. I'll be going back to work, and I need someone who can be here three to four days out of the week, depending on Jeanette's and my schedules."

"Oh yes, I understand. I am a retired pediatric nurse and just recently widowed, so I need the position to get me out of the house, plus supplement my income."

"How many years of experience do you have working with newborns?"

"Well, let's see. I've worked at Bon Secours St. Mary's Hospital for over fifteen years before I started to do private duty. I have a degree in nursing. I can tell you, I devote my life helping little ones because they are helpless at that age."

I sat there trying to listen and also analyze her to see if she showed any signs of craziness.

"Well, did you get fired or have any complaints filed against you?" Jeanette interrupted.

"Stop, I'm handling this."

"Hell, we need the truth. You must not watch the news. These crazy-ass people be hurting these babies."

"That's fine; I totally understand your friend's concern. I will be more than happy to answer all questions."

"Nah, you don't need to, and Jeanette is my mother, not my friend; please excuse her behavior," I said.

I then looked Jeanette dead in her eyes. She knew I was not playing. Azir was my child, and I could hire whoever the fuck I want.

"OK, OK, I'm gone." She stood up and put her hands in the air and pranced out.

"I'm sorry about that. Do you have a copy of your driver's license and the police record that I requested?"

She handed them to me. I wrote down her full name and address in my notebook. I had to be careful who I brought up in my house to watch over my angel.

"Well, I thought you were married. I hope I'm not prying."

"I'm not married, but I have a significant other who's out of town for a while."

"I see. He must be a special guy. Your face lit up as you spoke about him."

"Yes . . . Alijah *is* a special kind of guy. I really miss him; I can't wait for him to come home."

"My William was also a great guy. Unfortunately, the cancer took him away from me and the girls. We really miss him," she said while choking up.

"I'm sorry for your loss. I will keep you and your family in my prayers."

"Thanks, dear, it is so hard to find real love."

"Tell me about it. Alijah is my first love, and I went through hell and back just to have him, but I will say it was worth it," I said with a smile plastered on my face.

"He sounds like a winner. Hold on to him because these days, good men are so hard to find."

"I will."

There was something about her face that seemed so familiar, like we've met before. I tried to rack my brain. I just couldn't recall.

"Ms. Sadie, your face looks familiar. Have we met before?"

"Really? No, I'm good with faces, and I, my dear, would've remembered a pretty face like yours. You know the saying: we all have a twin running around," she chuckled.

"Yea, you right about that. OK, if you take the job, I will pay you four hundred per week."

"God bless you, my dear. I prayed for help, and here you are. I will definitely take care of your little gem."

"How soon can you start?"

"As soon as you want me to."

"How about tomorrow? I'll be here, but this will give you a chance to see how I do things, and you will get to meet Azir."

"Sure thing. I will be here bright and early."

"OK, great. Thank you. I look forward to having you around."

We sat around and talked for a little while; then she left. I was optimistic about the interview. She had the experience, plus her police record was clean. I had a feeling that Azir was going to be in great hands.

Chapter Eighteen

Sierra Rogers

The nanny was on time, which was a big plus in my eyes. Azir was wide awake, so I introduced him to her. She fell in love instantly.

"Oh my goodness, he is sooo handsome." Her eyes lit up bright like the sun. A part of me felt at ease.

"I take it he favors his daddy?"

"Yup, he looks just like him. The only thing he got from me is my nose."

"Babies are such a blessing. Can I hold him?"

"Sure." I handed Azir to her.

Our first day went smoothly. I paid full attention to the way she interacted with him. He was smiling from ear to ear as she rocked him. I peeped how relaxed he was when she sang "Jesus Loves Me." If I had any doubt about her before, they were erased. She was a good fit for him.

Jeanette, on the other hand, was not buying into that sweet old lady persona.

"Sierra, I'm telling you, there's something about that woman that ain't right. I just can't put my finger on it," she warned.

"Jeanette, let's be honest. You did not like that woman since the day she stepped foot in here. I have a feeling you're kind of jealous."

"Jealous? Hmm, there you go again attacking me. All I am saying is, don't let your guard down."

"Every time I say something, you accuse me of attacking you. Listen, lady, it's *my* son, so I can hire whoever the hell I want to. You're in *my* house, so you don't have to like her, but you *will* respect her while she's in here caring for my damn son."

"Excuse me, everybody knows by now that this is your house and he's your son. I didn't ask to come here, so if you don't want me here, just say it, instead of coming at me sideways. I might've fucked up, but I am not a fucking child, and I refuse to be treated like one!"

She walked off before I could get another word in. She was lucky that the woman was there and I wasn't going to put others in our business. I was mad because I really wanted to serve her ass.

***

It was Friday, and it was my second day at the salon. My first day back was great. Mo' and some of my clients surprised me when I walked through the door. It was really nice to see people that have been supporting the business from day one. I also enjoyed being in Mo's presence. We laughed and talked in between clients. The new girl Joslyn seemed cool. It was weird having another stylist around, but Mo' needed the help, and I wasn't back full time. For the time being, she served her purpose.

It's been almost a week since I've spoken to Alijah. I tried calling the jail, but all they would tell me was that he was still there. I called his lawyer to find out if he had an idea of what was going on. He informed me that Alijah was fine, and he wasn't sure why he wasn't calling home.

I waited for visitation day to roll around; then I drove up to the jail. I waited for them to call my name and was finally motioned to go to the desk . . . where I was informed that he was not accepting visitors. I stood there dumbfounded. Then I just turned around and walked out with my son.

See, this was the situation. I just drove forty-five minutes to go see that nigga, and that selfish-ass nigga denied my visit. I stormed off to my car. "God!" I did not know why I tried so hard to be a good woman to his sorry behind, and he still felt the need to carry me. I swear that I was tired of his bullshit.

I strapped my baby in his car seat and headed on down the road. I kept questioning God, and still no answer. I swore on my child from that day on I was going to focus on my son. I was done being Alijah's doormat. He really thought it was OK to turn off his feelings as he pleases. "Well, no fucking more," I said as I hit the steering wheel. I had spent my whole life crying, feeling abandoned, and used. Fuck that. I will not let another person think that they can do whatever they want with me. Well, Sierra Rogers has news for them. It was fucking over!

I stopped by the shop for a little. Mo' wanted to see her god-baby.

"Here's some clothes for him. I was at the mall yesterday, and I couldn't resist." She handed me the bag as soon as I entered the store.

As usual, she bought him some more clothes. This little boy was going to be spoiled. He already had too many clothes in his closet.

"Girl, if you buy another piece of clothing for this boy, I'm going to scream."

"You just jealous. That's *my* god-baby, and I will buy whatever I want. Ain't that right, sugar pooh?" she said while she tickled Azir.

"Sierra, you a'ight? You look like you been crying."

"Mo', I drove all the way cross the bridge to see this nigga, and he denied my visit," I said before I busted out crying.

"You serious? What kind of shit he's on?"

"Girl, I don't know, but I can't take no more."

"Sierra, you know I don't like when you get to crying. That is foul as hell. He must not know how much you out here holding him down."

"I'm just tired of it all. I try so hard to stand by him through all the drama, and it's like he don't give a damn."

"Sierra, you my bitch, so you know I'ma keep it one hundred. You too good of a woman to keep putting up with Alijah and his antics."

"It ain't even that. I love this nigga."

"Baby, I know you do, but you need to think about how this might turn out. He might be gone for good, and you still need to live your life. You young, pretty, sexy, and independent. Trust me, plenty niggas or bitches would love to wife you." She winked at me.

I busted out laughing.

"You're a fool for that. I am *not* gay; strictly dickly."

"Whatever, Sierra. You might not want to admit to or accept it, but I have news for you.

You love to get your pussy licked, and you love to lick pussy in return. You are a bisexual woman."

"Girl, you're joking around, but I'm hurting."

"I know it, bestie; was only trying to lighten the situation up a little. You know what you need to do. Don't stay in a relationship that cause you pain. You're better than that."

"I know, and I hear what you're saying, but it's not that easy to walk away from him. I love this man."

"Well then, dry them tears, put on your big-girl panties, and deal with it. It doesn't matter what you decide, I'll be right there with you."

"Thanks, *chica*. I'm tired, and I need to get Azir home and out of this cold. Thanks for listening to me without judging."

"No thanks needed. You my bestie, sister, and friend. No matter what happens in life, we have each other."

"Yea, I know."

I stood and wrapped up Azir in his thick blanket.

"Oh shit, I almost forgot. Did you hear Neisha is missing? Her mama and them been going around passing out flyers. Have you heard from her lately?"

"Nah, I haven't seen or talked to her since the day we fought," I lied. She really caught me off guard with that question, but I kept my composure.

"Girl, that is crazy. Well, I hope they find her, 'cause I know how tight y'all were."

"Yea, me too, but knowing Neisha, her ass will pop up soon."

"I hope so for her mama sake."

"A'ight, *chica,* I'm about to bounce. I'll be here around ten."

"OK. I'm about to close up. I already did my last head. Plus. I have a date with Malachi sexy ass. Girl, he is so damn fineee . . . *and* he paid, so you *know* I'm on it."

"Get it, boo."

"You know I am. I have a weakness for a sexy man and his money."

"Shit, I feel you on that. I'm allergic to broke-ass niggas. I just can't deal."

"Anyway, let me go. I love you."

"I love you too, *chica.* Give me a call when you reach home. Let me kiss my baby bye."

She kissed Azir, and I left. I need a change in my life—sooner than later.

Shayna Jackson

Things were really looking up for me after all the pain that I went through in the previous weeks.

I can honestly say things took a turn for the better. I would've never thought in a million years that I would be given this grand opportunity.

I had to give it to that federal bitch, because it was her brilliant idea, along with my Hollywood performance. "I swear to you I see an Academy Award in the making. Mrs. Shayna Jackson; best female actress!" I busted out laughing at that. See, that ho-ass bitch saw my husband and I, and somehow in that sick head, she felt like she could replace me. Only this time, she fucked the wrong nigga, and look at everything that was happening.

I would love to see the look on Alijah's face when he realized that he fucked up his life over a poor, underprivileged, stinking pussy. I tell you, men never learn. Well, no, in his case, he learned the *hard* way. Oh well, life goes on in the free world.

I poured me a glass of wine and cut on the slow jams. I was in the mood to celebrate my new job and my new mission.

"Cheers to me; the baddest bitch that ever walked these streets," I yelled as I raised my glass.

I drank two more glasses and got into bed. I had a long day ahead of me, and I needed all the rest that I can get in.

***

I looked in the mirror at my new appearance. I looked damn good to be a woman in my fifties. That makeup artist was the truth. Somehow, my new appearance reminded me of Mrs. Doubtfire. So ironic, I thought. That's my favorite movie that Alijah and I done watched over five times.

I never thought of becoming an actress, but after the way I performed when I applied for the job, I say I could get an award. I was actually sitting across from the whore that broke up my marriage, and it tickled me that she had no idea that it was me. She did ask if we met before. That kind of spooked me, but I remained calm, cool, and collected. The mother, on the other hand, was going to be a problem. I saw the way she kept looking at me as I spoke. I thought I was going to lose my cool when she started to question me, but luckily, her daughter jumped in. I had a feeling that bitch was not going to let up; however, she was in a run for her money because I was *that* bitch that she didn't want any kind of trouble with.

I gained Sierra's trust, and before long, I was taking care of her child. As I looked in his face, all I could see was Alijah. Our first day alone was very hard as I held him in my arms. I burst out crying. This was supposed to be Alijah's and my baby boy; instead, he killed mine, and now here he is with a baby with another bitch.

There were so many emotions running through me at the time that I came that close to suffocating the little bastard with his own pillow. Shit, I could've blamed it on SIDS. I would've loved to see the expression on his father's face when he learned that his baby Jesus had died. I bet money his ass would've burst out crying and carrying on just like he did when my baby passed. He had everyone around us fooled like he was mourning. That was all a show. His ass was too selfish to even care. I was buried so deep in my thoughts that I didn't know the grandma was approaching me until it was too late.

"What are you doing with that pillow, and why are you standing over my daughter's baby crying?"

"Ms. Jeanette! You startled me. I am so sorry. I was trying to put the pillow by the side of his crib for support."

"Yea, right, and you crying."

"Yes, I got news earlier that one of my cousins in Louisiana passed away."

"Mmm-hmm, whatever," she said while walking away.

I quickly wiped my tears. That was a close call. I straightened up my clothes and made sure the wire that I was wearing under my clothes was not visible. I left the room and went downstairs. That woman was becoming a nuisance, and I needed to get rid of her fast.

I had things to do before I headed to work, and I needed to make sure I didn't wear my wire today. Shoot, if the feds asked what happened, I'll just pretend like I forgot to wear it. I stopped on the corner of Broad Street. The young bums were posted selling their drugs of choice. I pulled over and bought me a forty bag of crack. I also stopped at the convenience store and bought a rose and a lighter. I sat in the car and burned the rose so it would look like it has been used. In less than twenty minutes, my mission was accomplished.

I headed to work and pulled up in the driveway. I was greeted at the door, as usual, by the very polite Sierra. We chatted for a little. Azir was asleep in her room, so I decided to do the laundry. I left Sierra downstairs and headed upstairs to get the baby's dirty laundry basket, and since he was asleep in his mom's bed, I decided to strip his mattress.

I waited two minutes . . . Then I ran hurriedly down the stairs into the kitchen.

"Ms. Sierra, I need to talk to you."

"What is it, Ms. Sadie? You look like you've seen a ghost."

"I was changing the sheet in the baby's crib, and when I took off his bedding, this fell out from under the sheet." I opened my hand to reveal the twenty-dollar bag of crack and the rose.

"What the hell is that?" She grabbed the package out of my hand.

"I'm no expert, but I believe it's crack and a pipe, ma'am."

"Oh, hell, no. You found this in my baby's crib?"

"Yes, ma'am. I don't mean to upset you. It's just dangerous for something like this to be in a baby's crib."

She pushed me out of the way and stepped to the foot of the stairs.

"Jeanette!"

"What, chile, all that darn hollering," Jeanette said as she walked down the stairs.

"You back getting high?"

"What? Sierra, it's too early for this shit."

"Goddamit, answer me."

"No, I'm not."

"So how the fuck did this get into my baby crib?" I grabbed her arm.

"Let go of me. I don't know how that got there. Why don't you ask *her?*"

"I am asking *you.* Ms. Sadie found it. I can't believe that I brought you in my house, and you still getting high."

"Baby girl, I 'ont know what's going on here, but Jesus is my witness; it's been over a year since I touched any kind of drugs."

"You're a fucking liar. You didn't change; I can't believe that I thought you did. You made a fucking fool out of me."

"Sierra, I swear to you I did *not* do it. I love Azir too much. I would never do that to him."

"Bitch! I don't believe shit that come out of your mouth. Get your shit and get out of my fucking house."

"Sierra, please believe me. I was set up. It ain't mine," she pleaded.

"You're pathetic. I gave you a place to stay for free, and *this* is the thanks I get. Don't you *ever* come near me again," Sierra warned.

I stood there as the situation played out. I never thought she would put her mother out, but it worked out great for me. At least I don't have to worry about that bitch breathing down my neck any longer, and I can really get into the reason I was there in the first place.

"Sierra, I am so sorry. I didn't mean to cause any type of fuss between you two."

"Ms. Sadie, you have nothing to be sorry about. I'm glad you found the drugs and brought it to my attention. She still would've been smoking, and God knows what would've happen to my son while in her care."

"Yes, I understand. We have to protect the babies, especially the ones that young."

A few minutes went by before Jeanette walked down the stairs with a few black trash bags in her hands. She placed them by the door and walked into the living room and approached me.

"You did this to me, you evil bitch! I see all through your lies. I promise you, whatever your motives are, if you even breathe too hard on my child and my grandchild, I will beat you down like a common bitch."

"I'm sorry you feel this way. I advise you to seek some help. Crack is a serious drug," I said, then got up and walked off.

Sierra must've heard her because she walked toward the door and opened it.

"Let's go. Stop blaming everyone else for your fuckup."

Jeanette grabbed her bags and stormed through the door while tears were rolling down her face.

"Watch that bitch with your baby."

"Bye, Jeanette, go live your life," Sierra said and closed the door.

I sensed that she was upset over the situation. She turned around and walked up the stairs.

"Yes! Mission accomplished," I mumbled under my breath.

Chapter Nineteen

Sierra Rogers

I really questioned God a lot. I want to know why I was cursed from the time of birth until now. I can't recall one time in life when I was happy without drama. After all the stress that I was going through with Alijah, it got even worse when the babysitter found crack cocaine in my baby's crib. I really thought Jeanette had changed and was no longer on drugs. Shit, that heifer behaved like she was enrolled in NA meetings. She had my black ass fooled.

I was grateful that Ms. Sadie found the drugs and her lies were uncovered. Now, I realized why she was so bent on me not hiring that lady; Jeanette had a huge secret. I'm going to be honest. I felt bad putting her out, but I had no choice. I was not going to allow a crackhead in my house and definitely *not* around my child. I would hate if I had to put my hands on her, so the best thing for both of us was to let her go. She kept telling me I was wrong, but I know her. That was a crackhead for you, though . . . always screaming they clean and they will try their hardest for you to see things their way. Also, I see the program wasn't helpful because the first step of recovery was acceptance.

Ms. Sadie became Azir's full-time nanny. I even had her staying over some days. I could see that she really enjoyed taking care of him. That helped put my mind at ease when I was gone for long hours. I admit, though, I called every thirty minutes to check up on him.

Alijah still hasn't called, but I spoke to his lawyer, and he gave me updates on his case. I wrote Alijah a few letters demanding some type of explanation to his madness. I was livid that he didn't call to check on his son.

I was OK in the daytime because I kept myself busy, but nights when Azir was asleep and I was alone, I cried my heart out. I love that man, and I wish none of that bullshit would've happened, and it's worse since he cut off our only way of communicating. I didn't care if he's locked up. When I do talk to him, I will be digging in his ass—trust that!

I had so many things to tackle. Top of the list was the safe with the money. I needed to get it out of the house, but I had no idea what I was going to do with it. I can't walk in a bank and deposit a few million, which would look suspicious. I had to figure something out soon. I wasn't too sure that the law was not investigating me, and I could not risk them running up in the house and confiscating the money. For the time being, my basement was the safest place, and I kept the door locked at all times.

One day I pulled up to my house just as soon as the mailman was delivering mail. He stopped at my box, so I got out of the car and took the mail from him. Most of it was bills and junk mail; there was also a letter from Alijah. I opened the front door, hurried up the stairs, and closed my bedroom door. I sat on the bed and opened the envelope. He started off apologizing for his actions, he wanted me to kiss his son, and then he got into how I should move on with my life because they're going to give him life. I was at a loss for words when I read the part where he told me that Saleem was a federal agent. *"Hell no!"* I screamed out. There's no way that was possible. He was Alijah's confidant and biggest supporter.

I was lost at that point; the game has no loyalty. In the letter, he also told me that he wrote me numerous letters without any reply. I was puzzled at that statement because this was the first letter I got since he decided not to have visits. He also explained that he wanted me to stay away because he did not want my name to be mixed up in all the things that were going on.

I sat on the edge of the bed crying. I knew he did lots of fucked-up things, but he did not deserve all that was being done to him. Most of his crew was snakes. They were out to bring him down, and they succeeded at it. I noticed he did not mention Shayna because she was the one that I was interested in, I was so ready to take that bitch on.

I dried my tears and walked downstairs and into the living room where Ms. Sadie was singing and rocking Azir.

"Hey, hon, how are you feeling?" Ms. Sadie asked out of concern.

I looked at her. "I'm fine. I want to ask you something. Have you been getting the mail from the mailbox?"

"I've only gotten the mail a few times, and I always placed it on the kitchen counter," Ms. Sadie answered quickly as she continued to rock Azir.

"OK, 'cause Azir's dad has been writing me, and I haven't gotten one letter."

"That's strange. It might be the neighborhood kids messing with your mail," she replied without skipping a beat.

"Yea, maybe. I've never had that problem before. OK, thanks."

"Anytime, dear."

There was something in my gut telling me that she wasn't being truthful. I've always kept my eyes on her face. There was something familiar about it. I wish I could remember where we've met before. She said we've never met, but I know we had. I just can't put my finger on it. Another thing that I've noticed was when I first interviewed her for the position she had a thick Southern accent. But earlier when I spoke to her, she had an up north accent. Hmm . . . two different accents—she's not fooling me. People only disguise their voice when they have something to hide.

Ms. Sadie, what's your story? What are you hiding? Whatever skeletons you have in your closet I will discover, one way or another.

Chapter Twenty

Alijah Jackson

My trial date was rapidly approaching. I decided to not accept any kind of plea deal that the government was offering. It was a fucking joke to me. They were offering thirty to forty-five years in federal prison *if* I plead guilty. Hell, nah! I wasn't copping out, even though I knew the odds were against me. I was willing to take my chances with the jurors. I was also going into it well aware that they had a 95-percent conviction rate. My lawyer was against going to trial, but what he wanted didn't really matter. It was my life, so I made the call.

I wrote Sierra multiple letters and got no response. I figured that she tight with a nigga because I didn't want a visit. Shit, that's how I was feeling. I'm a dude, but I was hurting inside. I decided to write her one last letter telling her that she needed to move on. Reality was I might be gone, so I didn't want to be locked down and have to worry about who she fucking or which nigga she had around my seed. It was best that I pull myself away before, so later, it won't be that hard for the either of us.

I spoke to Mom-dukes, and she was so heart-broken when I told her I was locked up. She cried through the entire conversation and told me she will be there for my trial. I ain't going to front; when I got back in my cell, I broke down. I hate to hear my mom cry, and it was harder now because I wasn't there to console her.

The rest of the day went by slowly, as usual; exercise, cards, and rapping with the homie was an everyday routine. Lights were out at eleven as usual. Whenever the block got quiet, my mind tends to race, and that night was no different.

I heard the guards holla "count time," and keys started to rattle. These motherfuckas never care if niggas were already asleep. They barge up on tier loud and disrespectful. I closed my eyes so I could let my mind wander far away from all the chaos. I heard my cell door pop open. I jumped on my feet but was blindsided by the bright lights from several flashlights. I felt a sharp jab in my left rib; a couple of others followed. Tape was placed over my mouth. I tried to fight back, but I was in no shape, and I was outnumbered. I began to lose lots of blood.

Shayna Jackson

The feds were riding my ass about getting more information about Sierra. They wanted something they could go after her with and also for me to get information about Alijah's money. The bitch barely spoke of her personal life, so how did they expect me to get that information? I had my own plan, though; I just had to figure a way to execute it without getting caught.

The other day I was alone, as usual, so I got to snooping. I was always curious about why the basement door stayed locked. I waited until Sierra left for work. I was happy that I knew how to pick locks, so I quickly opened the door and made my way down the stairs. I looked around; nothing was out of the ordinary. It was a finished basement. I was turning around to leave when I saw what looked like a door that was in a weird place for a closet. My curiosity got the best of me, so I opened the door—and there it was—a built-in hidden safe. I took a closer look and realized that unless I had the code, it was humanly impossible to pop it open. I had a feeling that was where Alijah had the majority of his money hidden. I closed the door and hurried back upstairs. I needed to figure out a way to get in that safe.

Sierra made it home, and I was eager to leave. I needed to get in my hotel where I could sit back and figure out a way to approach the situation. After all, I was still the legal missus, and I deserved *everything* that man owned—not that ho and her li'l bastard. We chatted for a little while before I left. Then I got into my car. I planned to go back the next day bright and early with a plan.

I arrived at the hotel, and, as usual, I had to call and check in with *them*. That bitch Rozarrio was still breathing down my neck like I was not doing enough.

"I need you to dig deeper in her life," she yelled.

"I don't know what you want me to do. I try talking to her, but she doesn't say much."

"Mrs. Jackson, I don't think you understand that it's either *you* or *her,* and I would want to think that you would choose the latter to go down."

"Listen, I'm tired of you holding that shit over my head. Why don't you get your ass in there and get whatever it is that *you* want for your damn self? I'm done dealing with you, so do whatever the fuck you want," I screamed.

"Lower your voice," Rozarrio fired back. "This is an order! I will throw your ass in jail and won't think twice about it. You have one damn week to get in there and get me the information about where all Alijah's money is and how much information she knew about his business. You have until five o'clock Friday evening," she said and hung up the phone.

That bitch done lost her mind talking to me like that. I will be calling her damn supervisor. I won't tolerate her or anyone else disrespecting me. I was not going to get her shit. I had my own plans for Sierra, and handing her and Alijah's money over to them was not my intention.

I poured a glass of wine and got Mr. Mandingo out of the drawer and put some K-Y Jelly on him. Then I opened my legs wide and fucked myself for a good thirty minutes, busting all over it, and then crawled up underneath my blanket. I was beat.

Chapter Twenty-One

Sierra Rogers

It was the weekend, and I decided to stay home. I was trying to find someone else to watch Azir. There was something about Ms. Sadie that rubbed me the wrong way. I picked up she was lying about not getting my letters and her accent being switched up between the North and the South. She portrayed herself as that sweet old lady, but when I watch her walk, she walked like she has no ailment. I was waiting for her to come in that Monday so I could sit down and have a talk with her. I needed to get to the bottom of why she was disguising herself. I prayed to God she had an explanation because I would hate if I had to hurt that woman.

The phone rang once, rang a few more times, and I ignored it, thinking the person would get the drift. Obviously, they did not get the memo, because they kept calling. I rolled over and snatched the phone off the nightstand. "I'ma cuss this motherfucker out," I mumbled under my breath as I picked up the phone.

"Hello," I answered in a high tone.

"Sorry to wake you up, Ms. Rogers, but I want to inform you that there was an incident at the jail, and Alijah was hurt."

The caller had my full attention now. I jumped up out of bed onto the floor.

"What the fuck you mean? Is he all right? Is he dead?"

"I don't have the full details. The U.S. attorney called me since Alijah's my client. He is in serious condition and is on the way to MCV as we speak."

"Oh my fucking God, this can't be happening again," I said, then hung up in dude's face.

I was already crying by the time I hung up. My memories took me back to when he got shot. I was feeling the same kind of emotions. The difference was, this time, I was not beside him holding his hand. He was locked up, and I was out here. My thoughts were bundled, and I couldn't think straight. I need to get to MCV ASAP, which might be a waste of time because he was locked up, and I am pretty sure that they would have him under high security.

I was pacing back and forth like a dopefiend. I need to know what to do. I dialed Mo's phone. There was no answer. I know she was asleep. I looked at the time. It was a little after 2:00 a.m. I didn't know who else to call. I scrolled to Jeanette's number and dialed it. After the first ring I was tempted to hang up, but I needed her like no other.

"Hello," she whispered into the receiver.

"Hey, sorry to wake you. I'll call back later."

"Sierra, what's wrong? You're crying."

"Yes, something bad happened to Alijah at the jail."

"What you talking 'bout, chile? Have you been drinking?"

"No, Mama." The word slipped out of my mouth, and I only realized it after it was too late.

"Baby girl, I'm here for you. Are they sure it's him? I mean, how could that happen to him?"

"I don't know anything," I said with aggravation in my voice.

"OK, Sierra, I'll be over there after my NA meeting this morning, but if you need me, don't hesitate to call me."

"Right," I said and hung up.

I dialed Mo's number again, but still no answer. Then I dialed the lawyer's number.

"Ms. Rogers, I was just going to call you back. The jail confirmed that he was stabbed multiple times and was transferred to the hospital. I tried to reach the U.S. attorney but was not able to. I have to be in court this morning with another client, so I'll be heading to the hospital after that."

"So is he alive? How bad is it?"

"Not sure. The hospital is not giving out any information on him."

"OK, this is bullshit. They acting like he don't have no fucking family. I hate this fucking system."

"I understand, but I want you to know I'm on top of it and will get back with you as soon as I know something."

I hung up the phone and grabbed my pillow. Lord knows my heart can't take any more. I hope he makes it. I don't want to lose him. My son needs his father. I cried out loud, tears flowing down. I just can't take any more of it. My strength is gone. I wanted to die!

Alijah Jackson

Everything around me was bland. I was going in and out of consciousness, but I tried to get an understanding of what was going on around me.

I knew I got stabbed a few times with a sharp object. The first thought that came to mind was it's a hit on my life; however, I was confused why they didn't just kill me. I wasn't sure who was behind the attack, but I wasn't a fool. It was an inside job. It wasn't like it was daytime and I got into it with another nigga. This was in the middle of the night, and the cell was popped. The guards were the only ones that could pop a cell from their office.

I didn't recognize the faces of the niggas that stabbed me, or I was too confused to make sense of it all. I knew I was in an ambulance and somebody was patching me up. They had my eyes blindfold at this point, so there was nothing I could see.

The ambulance came to a stop, and I lay there scared to breathe. I had no idea what was about to happen. I heard niggas talking back and forth.

"OK, this is it right here," I heard a nigga with poor English yell out.

"Yeah, the boss said pull over right here," another one answered.

I whispered a prayer to God. I knew this was the end for me. My son, my mama, and Sierra flashed across my mind, and silent tears rolled down my face. I then felt someone approach me.

"Youngblood, get yo' ass up."

I immediately recognized Saleem's voice. He took off the blindfold and the duct tape my mouth. I could barely move, but I stood up in the ambulance. I went to rush him with the little strength I had but fell short.

"Yo' pussy hole snitch bwoy, what the fuck going on? Why am I here?"

"Easy, brother. I know you tight with me, but we do not have the time to catfight. We have to go now."

"I ain't no fuckin' fool. You is an informant that I trusted with my life. Why the fuck you think I would trust you now? Hell, nah."

"I don't give a fuck 'bout you trusting me. You can stay and go to prison for life, or you can take your chances and bring yo' ass to the plane that's waiting to take us out of the country. The choice is yours."

At that moment I was lost as fuck. I wanted to go, but how can I trust this nigga? He's the law.

"Man, you wasting time; here, take the phone. Call Sierra and let her know that Shayna is working undercover as the nanny. Do it now 'cause we need to get rid of the phone," Saleem commanded as he pushed the phone in my hand.

I snatched the phone and dialed Sierra's number. He threw my arm over his shoulder. He was giving me support because I was still in pain from the stabs. The phone rang and rang, but no answer. I ended up leaving her a voice mail in hope that she would check it. How the hell did Shayna pull that one off? Then I remembered the fucking law was behind it all.

We made our way through a long-ass tunnel. All kinds of crazy thoughts invaded my mind. This nigga was the feds. Why was he helping me to escape?

"Yo, B, you the motherfucking law, so why you doing this to help li'l ole me?"

"Brother, I told you from day one, I gotcha. You will never understand it now, but when we get to our destination and things are settled, I will explain everything; then, you will under-stand better. Now, let's go. We have less than a minute."

We made it to the end of the tunnel, and I saw that a one-engine Cessna was waiting in the field. He let me go, and I tried to hop on my own. Out of nowhere, a big helicopter flew over us. Feds came out of every corner with guns drawn.

"Alijah Jackson and Agent Coleman, don't move!"

We both looked at each other. No words were needed. We were going to make a run for it. We sprinted off; Saleem was ahead of me because of the severe pain that I was in.

"I said don't fucking move!" a voice yelled before shots were fired.

I saw Saleem get shot, but it didn't stop him. I was just thinking a few more steps and I will be free—free of all the drama. I would be in a new country.

The first bullet hit me in the leg, but I continued to run.

"Come on, brother, I got you." He grabbed my hand, and we both made a run for it.

The second bullet hit me in my lower back. I still didn't go down. I tried to drag my leg one more step to freedom.

A few bullets flew by my ear and hit Saleem's body. He went down in slow motion. I tried to drag him with me. He looked at me and shook his head no.

"Go on!" he barely mumbled.

I tried to take a few more steps to the plane. Five more bullets ripped through my slender body, and one lodged into the back of my neck. I tasted blood in my mouth and fell to the ground.

Chapter Twenty-Two

Sierra Rogers

I cried all morning and waited to get a phone call about Alijah's situation. I called the jail and the hospital but couldn't get anything from them. They were behaving like it was classified information. It was around 6:00 a.m. I decided to take a shower. I needed to take my ass to MCV and ask to speak to a supervisor. Ms. Sadie was scheduled to watch Azir, and even though I was going to have a serious talk with her, it would have to wait until I see what's going on with Alijah.

I showered, got dressed, and waited. She walked in five minutes to nine.

"Good morning, my dear child."

"Good morning. Azir is asleep, and I have some errands that I have to run. I'll be back in a few," I said and hurried out the door.

I got into my car. I was heading to MCV, which was the hospital where the lawyer said they were taking him. I hope I don't have to go down there and act a fucking fool. I knew I wasn't married to him, but I had his damn child, and that should count for something.

I got through all the traffic that was on the streets on a Monday morning. I really hated to drive behind those slow-ass school buses. If it wasn't against the law and the little camera that they had installed on the side I would definitely go around them when they stopped. I finally made it to the hospital and parked my car. It was cold outside, and because I wasn't thinking rationally, I ran out of the house without my jacket. I took long strides until I hit the hospital lobby.

I approached the front desk.

"Hello, good morning. I'm here to visit Alijah Jackson."

"Good morning, ma'am. Let me check that patient information for you." His fingers pounded the keys as he looked on the screen. Once his fingers stopped, he looked at me. "Sorry, ma'am, there's no one here with that name."

"What you mean? He was transferred here from Tappahannock Regional Jail earlier."

"I'll check again for you." The man banged the keys again. "Same thing, there is no patient here with that name," he confirmed.

"Man, you are not doing something right. I *know* he's here. I need your supervisor."

"OK, ma'am, he'll be in later on this morning."

"*Man, fuck you, you stupid bitch!*" I yelled out.

I walked away from the desk. Where the hell is Alijah? I looked at my phone to see what time it was. That's when I saw that I had over ten missed calls from an unfamiliar number. I stepped outside and called the number back. It went straight to voice mail. I tried it a few more times. I then saw that I had a new voice mail, so I dialed my voice mail.

"*Sierra, this me. I hope you're there. That bitch that you just hired is Shayna disguised as a nanny. Get out of there now. Please protect my son. I'll call you later. I love you and my seed. Don't mention this call to anyone. I love you, babes.*" I pressed 3 to listen to the message again.

Then I ran to my car, jumped in, and pulled off. I almost hit a few cars as I sped out of the parking lot. I tried to dial the number the nanny gave me, but it went straight to voice mail. I thought about calling the cops, but I didn't want to take a chance on her disappearing with my baby. I was confused. Alijah was supposed to be stabbed and in serious condition, but he left me a message an hour and a half ago. How did he know that Ms. Sadie was an imposter? God knows I just need to get home to my baby.

I cut the radio on to get my mind off what I was going to do. That's when the radio station reported that there was a sophisticated jail break at the jail in Warsaw. They also went on to say that Alijah Jackson was the federal inmate on the loose. He was armed and dangerous and should not be approached if seen. I turned off the radio as tears filled my eyes. I knew I would never see my man again. He was a marked black man out there!

I couldn't think straight after hearing the news about Alijah, but I couldn't focus on him. I had to focus on my son. I knew that I was heading home with one intention, and that was to kill this bitch. This bitch shot me, disguised herself as a nanny, and was up in my house with my son. There was no other option. I will protect me and mine until I took my last breath. Something else flashed in my mind. Was Jeanette really getting high, or did that bitch plant that evidence? I hit the steering wheel. I let a bitch play me again—and I fell for it.

I drove like a menace into the neighborhood and pulled up at the house. I tried to calm down a little so I could get in without giving off any vibes that I knew who she was. I took my gun out of my purse and tucked it in the waist of my jeans. Then I pulled my sweater down to disguise it. I opened the door and entered as usual and walked in.

Shayna Jackson

The weekend came and went by fast. Monday was always my best day of the week, but that Monday morning was my best one so far. I had a lot of things to get done once and for all. I woke up early and got dressed in some slacks and a nice cotton sweater. I need to feel comfortable because I never knew what might pop off.

I called Rozzario and let her know that I was not going to work; pretended as if I was too sick. After that, I gathered my gun and bullets, just in case the situation became a bloodbath. I made sure all my things were packed; then I put them into the trunk of the car. I had no intention to go back to the hotel.

Azir and I will be on our way after I kill his mommy. I thought about killing the bastard too, but I decided to keep him since he reminds me of Alijah, and also so he can become my little bastard. I couldn't wait to see the look on Sierra's face when she realizes that we have indeed met before. I cut the music up loud as I drove to claim what's rightfully mine.

I got there just in time for me to start working. I noticed upon my arrival the woman of the house looked a little agitated and tired. I was going to inquire about what was going on, but I refrained. I was on a mission, and I really didn't give a damn about what she was going through. I needed her to hurry up and leave so I could get to that safe. I figured I could shoot it open and see what they had been hiding in the basement. I planned to be gone long before she made it back home.

I watched as she hurried off and waited around twenty-five minutes until I was confident enough that she was gone. Then I picked the door that led to the basement and jogged down the stairs to the door that led to the safe. I fired two shots in the direction of the lock, hitting my target. The lock disabled; I took it off so I could open the safe.

I almost fainted. I leaned on the wall for support. I'd been with Alijah for years, and

I have *never* seen this substantial amount of money. The blasted man was rich, and these federal clowns thought they confiscated all of his bank accounts and monies. He was sitting on a gold mine, and this bitch thought she was going to run me off. "Ha-ha, silly rabbit." I bust out laughing. I couldn't contain myself.

I was no fool. There was no way I could drag all that money out, so I decided to grab a large black trash bag from out of the kitchen cabinet. I went back downstairs and started piling up stacks of cash. It took me a good while to fill up the bag. See, what I didn't bargain for was how heavy the bags were going to be. I couldn't even move an inch with it. I had to grab another bag and split the first bag. I made it upstairs with the two bags and took them to my car. I scanned my surroundings to make sure no one was spying on me.

Quickly, I went back into the house and headed upstairs. I grabbed some of Azir's clothes and packed them in a duffel bag that I found in the closet. I then went to his crib where he was lying. I wasn't going to get him dressed. I did not want to delay one second after I blew his mommy's brains all over her room. However, my thoughts were quickly interrupted.

Sierra Rogers

I tiptoed on my plush carpet which managed to drown out the squeaky noise of the stairs. I had my gun hidden behind my back. My heart was speeding because of the inevitable. I went directly to my room and stood in the doorway where I had a clear view of her standing over my son.

"*Get the fuck away from him!*" I yelled, with the gun pointed directly at her.

"Chile, put away that thing before you hurt yourself." She grinned.

"Shayna, that's your real name, right? Get the fuck away from my son."

"Ha! You got me, but please put your gun down, or I *will* shoot this little monkey," she said as she picked Azir up and pointed her gun at his face.

My heart skipped a couple of beats. I see this bitch had no heart; she would go that far and point a gun at my baby. My blood was boiling. I wanted to choke the life out of her, but I did not want to startle her. I was not sure of her mental state—one wrong move on my behalf could trigger her to do something stupid.

"OK, OK, take the gun off my baby. What do you want?"

"What I want? I see I missed when I shot you before. So here we are again."

"I understand that you are upset. Please take the gun off my baby," I pleaded while tears rolled down my face.

"I don't give a fuck about you pleading. You came into my life and wreaked my marriage. You didn't care then, so why the fuck you think I give a fuck about you or this little monkey?"

"Listen, I'll walk away. You can have Alijah. I'll leave him alone."

"Ha-ha, you one funny bitch. You thought it was a game. I never knew what he saw in a poor-ass bitch like you. Look at yo' ass. You look like a cheap ho on a cold night."

I stood there ignoring everything that the deranged ho was saying. My mind was set on getting my son out of her arms.

"You thought you were going to have him for you and this little bastard. Surprise! You thought wrong, bitch. Alijah belongs to me, *'til death do us part*. You get that?" she yelled. "He was *my* man. You had no right to weasel yourself into our lives. He was *mine!*" She started to cry.

"Please, I'm begging you, put my baby down," I pleaded with her.

The situation was definitely getting out of hand. This was any mother's worst nightmare.

I whispered a prayer to God and leaped toward that bitch. I was going to get my baby.

Pop! Pop! Pop! Pop! Shots fired off in my direction.

I didn't shoot back in fear of hitting my son. I fell right by his crib. I was trying to take a quick glance at my baby's face one last time.

"See, bitch, I told you to leave us alone, and you didn't listen."

Moments later, I heard footsteps, lots of them, running up the stairs.

"Sierra, can you hear me? Oh my God! Get an ambulance here right now," Jeanette yelled. "Baby, hold on, please. I can't lose you. Azir needs you," she pleaded.

I knew I was dying. I wanted to hold my baby for one last time. Just one last time.

"Baby, please hold on. Help is on the way. I love you." She cried as she hugged my bullet-riddled body.

"Please take care of my baby. Please let him know that I love him."

"You will be here to tell him yourself. Don't you talk like that, you hear me?" She hugged my bloody body.

I squeezed her hand as I dozed off. I knew this was my last time seeing the woman that gave me life. The breath was leaving my body, and I was going home to Grandma. I closed my eyes and breathed in deeply. My level of consciousness diminished, and my body started to shiver. I began to breathe rapidly as the pain became unbearable. I wasn't ready to go. I was feeling scared and lonely. I wanted Alijah and my son by my side.

"The ambulance is here. Let's go people! We need to get her to the hospital."

"Oh, somebody done done me wrong (Done Me Wrong). My eyes to the ceiling all night long (All night long) Time is slippin' away from me (Away from me) And it ain't no tellin' when I get home, I gotta get home, yeah." K-Ci & JoJo lyrics played in my mind.

"Come on, sugar, Grandmamma is here. You are safe now," she said as I collapsed in her arms.

Shayna Jackson

I thought I had everything under control after I got the money. I just needed to wait until she came home; then I would kill her and leave. But the plan changed. She popped up on me, and when she did, she already knew who I was. So I see she was smarter than I thought.

People might think I was a fool because I was fighting for a man that doesn't even want me, but we weren't always like that. We had a bond; we said *till death do us part*. I was supposed to be his everything, but he let an underprivileged bitch come between us. I wasn't fighting over him; I was fighting to get my respect. If I let that one bitch come in and fuck up my marriage, that will only open the door for all the other man-snatchers who think they can.

That ho had the audacity to pull a gun on me. I had to show her that I wouldn't think twice about blowing that little monkey's brains out. She was no match for me. I didn't care that he was young; the sin of the mother carries over to him. Her ass realized fast that I was dead-ass serious. The big bad Sierra vanished, and the little poor bitch that I knew she was appeared, begging me not to hurt her baby.

I already knew I was going to kill her, so when she leaped at me, I pulled the trigger and lit that black ass up while I held her son in the other hand. I was getting ready to put one in her brain, but I needed to get out of there. I grabbed the boy and ran down the stairs, but stopped in my tracks when I heard the front door breaking down. I knew right then it was the police, but who called them?

I thought I had it all figured out until the feds burst in the room and demanded that I put the gun down. I had no idea they knew where I was. I left the microphone at home, and I told them I was ill. I thought I was slick, but I guess they never trusted me. I see they were playing me just like I thought I was playing them. I had no intention to go to jail. I was not made for that; instead, I made the decision to end it all. I held Azir close to me; then I lunged forward, shooting at Agent Rozzario. She returned fire. Surprisingly, I was only shot in the shoulder. She ran over to me and snatched the little bastard out of my arm. The room flooded with agents.

A few of them rushed me up against the wall.

"Shayna Jackson, you are under arrest. You have the right to remain silent; anything you say can and will be used against you in a court of law. You have the right to an attorney, and if you cannot afford an attorney, one will be appointed to represent you. You can choose to exercise these rights at any time." Agent Rozzario read me my rights as she cuffed me.

"Bitch, you should've killed me." I looked her in the eyes.

"No, that'd be too easy. I will make sure you *rot* in prison for the rest of your life."

"Fuck you, bitch. I won't do a single day. You need me to testify against Alijah," I spat.

"I am sorry to inform you, Mr. Jackson was killed this morning, and I don't need you for a damn thing."

That was the second-worst news that I heard in my life. The first was the death of my daddy. I wonder if that bitch was bluffing, but then again, what if she wasn't? That would mean that I would be convicted of murder. Oh well, at least I knew Alijah and his ho would never see another day. I couldn't help but burst out laughing as they led me out of the house.

I saw the news station vehicles and all the neighbors crowded around. I hope I still looked damn good for my role. I pushed out my chest and held my head high. After all, I was the *head bitch in charge!*

The End